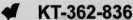

KT-362-836

CONTENTS

TEDDY BEAR TALES

FAIRY TALES

ANIMAL TALES

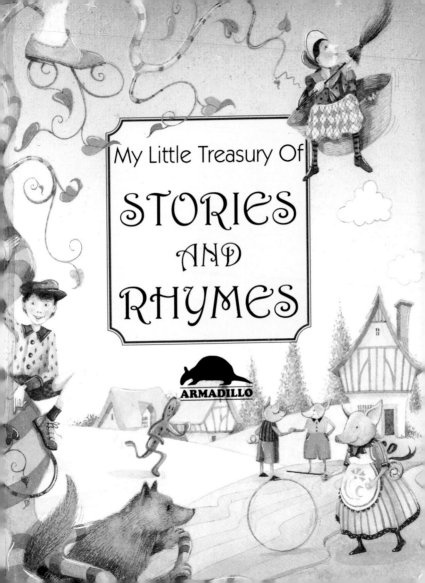

My Little Treasury Of

STORIES

AND

RHYMES

ARMADILLO

Illustrations by
Martine Blaney
Jo Davies
Francesca Duffield
Colin and Moira Maclean
Jenny Press
Terry Rogers
Cathie Shuttleworth
Lesley Smith
Annabel Spenceley
Jenny Thorne
Jenny Williams
Linda Worrall

This paperback edition published in 2005 by
Armadillo Books
An imprint of Bookmart Limited
Registered Number 2372865
Trading as Bookmart Limited
Blaby Road, Wigston, Leicestershire, LE18 4SE

10 9 8 7 6 5 4 3 2 1

ISBN 1-84322-432-1

Published in 1996 in a hardback format
Originally published in 1994 by Bookmart Limited as
My Treasury of Stories and Rhymes

Printed in Singapore

A CHRISTMAS TREASURY

TEDDY BEAR
TALES

The Teddy Bears' Picnic

Bears often decide to have picnics, and just as often, things don't go exactly according to plan. Once ten little bears planned a picnic.

One little bear tried to catch a butterfly and didn't come back for hours. Another attempted a somersault, and couldn't get up again.

The third bear went swimming, when he should have been helping. The fourth got the hiccups and was no use at all. The fifth bear fell asleep.

The sixth little bear was stung on the nose by a bee,

because he wondered if its honey might be tasty. The seventh got so excited that she had to have a rest! Her sister was chased by a crab. She forgot all about making sandwiches.

It was not surprising that the ninth little teddy bear decided to go home. So the tenth bear tucked into the buns and cakes all on his own, and was soon a very full little bear indeed!

At last, all the little bears did gather together for their party, but after all the excitement, they fell fast asleep ... every one of them!

Goldilocks and the Three Bears

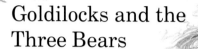

Once upon a time there was a very naughty little girl called Goldilocks. One day she went for a walk in the woods and found a little cottage. The front door was open, and Goldilocks went in!

In the kitchen, the little girl saw three bowls of porridge. Feeling hungry, she took a spoonful of the porridge in the biggest bowl.

"Ugh!" she said. "That is far too hot!"

She tried the next bowl. "Ugh! That is too cold!"

Finally Goldilocks tried the smallest bowl. She

didn't say a word – she was too busy
eating! The porridge was just right.

When she had finished, Goldilocks
looked for somewhere to sit down. In
the living room were three chairs.
She tried the big one first, but it was
far too hard. Then she tried the middle-
sized chair. But she didn't like that
one either. At last Goldilocks sat in
the little chair. It felt just right, but
... crash! ... Goldilocks was *too* heavy!

"I need a rest," said Goldilocks,
going upstairs to the bedroom.
She climbed onto the largest bed, but
it was too hard to sleep on.
Next she tried the middle-sized bed,
but that was too soft. So Goldilocks
tried the smallest bed. It was perfect!
Goldilocks fell fast asleep.

Just then, the three bears who
lived in the cottage came back from
their walk. At once they saw that
something was wrong.

"Who's been eating *my* porridge?"
asked Father Bear in a growly voice.

"Who's been eating *my* porridge?"
asked Mother Bear in a soft voice.

"And who's eaten *my* porridge –
all of it?" squealed Baby Bear.

In the living room, it was the same story. *Someone* had been sitting on each of the three chairs.

"Follow me," said Father Bear sternly, and he tiptoed up the stairs. "Someone's been lying on *my* bed!" he exclaimed.

"And someone's been lying on *my* bed," said Mother Bear.

"And someone's been sleeping in *my* bed," squeaked Baby Bear, "and she's still there! Look!"

At that moment Goldilocks woke up to see three angry, furry faces. She jumped up and ran straight home. And she never was *quite* so naughty again.

The Teddy Bear Who Had No Clothes

Little Katya had a very special birthday present.

"I'll call you Teddy Thomson," she told her new bear.

Next morning, when Katya went to school, she had to leave Thomson behind. He looked forward to meeting the other toys. But as soon as Katya had gone, he heard them giggling.

"I can hardly look. It's so *embarrassing*!" said the rag doll.

"It shouldn't be allowed!" giggled the baby doll.

"At least I have paint!" puffed the big blue train, blowing his whistle.

"I feel sorry for him really," said the clown.

Teddy Thomson couldn't think what they were talking about.

"My dear, surely you *know*!" gasped the rag doll. "You haven't any clothes on!"

"You're a *bare* bear!" chortled the train. "We can't play with you if you don't wear *something*."

Suddenly Teddy Thomson felt really silly. "What are teddy bears like me *supposed* to wear?" he asked.

The rag doll hunted in the toy box. "Here's my best dress," she said. "The one I wear for parties. You can wear it instead."

So Thomson put on the dress, which really fit him quite well. Then he looked in the mirror.

"Nothing in the world will make me wear this," he said firmly.

"I've got a spare suit," said the clown, helpfully. "And a slightly squashed spare red nose."

So Teddy Thomson put on the suit and the nose and went to the mirror again. "This is even *worse*," he cried.

"I've got something that suits everyone!" giggled the baby doll, handing Teddy Thomson a square of white material.

"Never!' growled Thomson.

"Then there's only one thing left," chugged the train. "We must paint you!"

Half an hour later, when Katya came home from school and saw Teddy Thomson, she burst into tears. "What's happened to your beautiful fur?" she cried.

So Katya bathed her teddy bear and took him outside to dry. And Teddy Thomson, deciding that he didn't *need* clothes or paint to cover his beautiful fur, sang a little song:

> "A bear isn't bare
> If he's wearing his fur.
> He's not at his best
> In a clown suit or dress.
> Being covered in paint,
> I'm bound to declare it,
> Was simply not *me*.
> I just couldn't BEAR it!"

The Big Bad Bear

"You can play wherever you like in the woods," said Mrs. Bear to her twins, "but what ever you do, don't disturb the Big Bad Bear!"

"What is a Big Bad Bear like?" whispered Buttons to his sister.

"He's big and … he's bad … and he's … a kind of bear," said Lily. "And I think I see him! Run!"

But when they had finished running, she thought that perhaps she had only seen a bear-shaped bush after all.

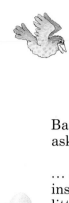

"What do Big Bad Bears eat?" asked Lily.

"Oh … berries … and nuts … and insects … and … little bears," said Buttons. "And I think I can hear him coming! Run!"

But when they had finished running, he thought that perhaps he had only heard the wind after all.

"What does a Big Bad Bear look like?" asked Buttons, nervously.

"He is very tall … and he has very big teeth … and he has very long claws," said Lily. "And I think I see him behind that tree! Run!"

But when they had finished running, she thought that perhaps it was only a bird in a tree after all.

Lily listened and noticed that the birds weren't singing. The leaves weren't rustling. There were no scampering, scuttling noises at all.

"It's *too* quiet," she said. "And I think I can see someone coming! Run!"

The two little bears ran until they were gasping for breath and could hardly see where they were going. Then ... crash! ... they fell over something lying under a tree.

Lily screamed, "Aaagh!"

Buttons yelled, "Aaagh!"

And the Big Bad Bear saw them both and shouted, "Aaagh!"

Then they all looked surprised.

"You're not very big and you don't look very bad," said Lily to the Big Bad Bear.

"I'm *not*!" said the little bear. "That's just my name."

"That's silly!" said Lily. "Names and bears should be alike."

The Big Bad Bear laughed. "You're right," he said. "Let's play. But first, what are *your* names?"

Tall Tree Trouble

There is one very important thing to remember if you are going to climb a tree – you have to be able to get down again. It's a pity that Teddy Bellingham didn't think of that before he set out one morning to climb the tallest tree in the garden.

It was harder than he had thought it would be. For one thing, the branches didn't seem to be in quite the right places. "This is a badly designed tree, from a climbing point of view," said the bear to himself, as he struggled to reach the next branch. After a few more branches, he was very tired indeed.

Teddy B. decided that it was time to have an official rest. In fact, he'd had a few *unofficial* rests already. He sat on a branch and swung his legs and looked down at the garden. It was a mistake. When the little bear looked down, he really couldn't help noticing what a *very* long way from the ground he was.

But Teddy B. was a brave little bear, so on he went, paw over paw toward the top.

It wasn't until his next official rest that Teddy Bellingham noticed that the tree was *moving*.

"Ooooh," moaned Teddy Bellingham, "I'm beginning to feel just a little bit queasy."

It was time for even a very brave bear to head for home. Poor Teddy Bellingham managed a few branches but then he had to admit, he was well and truly *stuck*. He sat on his branch for a long time. A cold, worried feeling grew in his tummy.

"No one knows I'm here," he thought. "I could stay here for ever!"

Suddenly Teddy B. noticed that the branch he was sitting on grew straight toward the house.

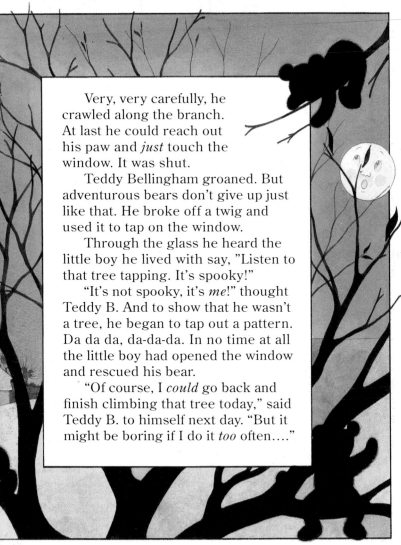

Very, very carefully, he crawled along the branch. At last he could reach out his paw and *just* touch the window. It was shut.

Teddy Bellingham groaned. But adventurous bears don't give up just like that. He broke off a twig and used it to tap on the window.

Through the glass he heard the little boy he lived with say, "Listen to that tree tapping. It's spooky!"

"It's not spooky, it's *me!*" thought Teddy B. And to show that he wasn't a tree, he began to tap out a pattern. Da da da, da-da-da. In no time at all the little boy had opened the window and rescued his bear.

"Of course, I *could* go back and finish climbing that tree today," said Teddy B. to himself next day. "But it might be boring if I do it *too* often...."

The Little Lost Bear

Once upon a time there was a teddy bear who kept getting lost. He fell behind the shelf in the toy shop and by the time he was found, Christmas was over and all the other bears had gone to good homes.

But one day, a man came in who was on a business trip. He wanted to take a present home for his little girl.

"This little bear is just what I need!" cried the man. "Elise has been wanting a bear like this for ages."

He tucked the little teddy bear
into his coat pocket and got back into
his taxi. But the man arrived late at
the airport and had to run to catch
his plane. As he ran, the little bear
fell out of his pocket.

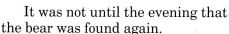

It was not until the evening that
the bear was found again.

"Just look!" said a smiling woman
in blue overalls. "This teddy bear will
be perfect for my little
nephew." She put him in
one of the pockets of her
overalls. But that night,
she threw her overalls into
the washing machine
without thinking.

Swoosh woosh! Soon the little bear was cleaner than he had ever been in his life! In the morning, the smiling woman's husband went outside to hang out the washing. No sooner had he put down the laundry basket, than a naughty puppy came along and carried the little bear off in his mouth. Puppies love to bury things, but the puppy's owner saw him starting to dig and cried out, "No, Bouncer!"

The puppy dropped the little bear and ran to his owner. A minute later, a seagull swooped down and picked the bear up in its beak.

This seagull soon got tired of carrying the little bear. It flew over the sea and dropped the little bear onto the deck of a cargo ship below.

"Well," said the captain. "I'll keep this little bear in my cabin."

When the ship at last arrived at port, the captain went to visit his sister in a nearby town, taking the bear with him. As he walked down the path, his niece ran to meet him.

"Uncle George!" she cried. "Have *you* brought me a present? Daddy forgot last time *he* went away."

The captain held out the little bear.

"Here you are, Elise," he laughed.

There's a Bear in the Bathroom!

"Hey!" yelled Charlie one evening.
"There's a bear in the bathroom!"

"Charlie!" shouted his mother.
"I've got enough to do looking after
the baby, without listening to silly
stories from you."

The bear smiled at Charlie.

Charlie looked carefully at the very large bear. "*What*," he said, "are you doing in our bathroom?"

"It's a very *nice* bathroom," said the bear in a low and growly voice.

"But how did you get here?" asked Charlie. The bear didn't answer but it looked a little guiltily toward the window, and Charlie could see some pretty large paw prints on the window sill.

"You can't stay here," he said to the bear. "You'd better come into my room."

"That's awfully kind of you," said the bear. "I don't suppose you have any ... er ... little snacks?"

Charlie took the bear to his room and gave him a half-eaten bag of soggy potato chips.

"Were you planning to stay long?" he asked, politely.

"If you like," replied the bear with a smile. "I thought perhaps you might like some company at the moment."

Charlie sighed.

It was true. Ever since his little baby brother had been born a few weeks before, it seemed that no one had any time for *him*. Charlie didn't like the baby. All day long it dribbled or cried. If *he'd* done that, he'd have been sent up to bed.

"I'm very glad you've come," said Charlie to the bear. "But you're going to have to be careful not to be found."

"I'll blend into the background," said the bear.

Charlie was doubtful, but in fact the bear turned out to be rather good at hiding himself.

Before long, Charlie and the bear became very good friends. Everyone else could make a fuss of the baby: Charlie had a special pal. When he was sad, the bear gave him a big furry hug. When he was happy, it made funny bear-faces that made Charlie laugh so much his tummy ached.

One day, Charlie went downstairs to find some apples for the bear and got a surprise. In the living room, his little brother was standing up!

He looked up, smiling all over his little face, and said, "Charlie!"

"Yes," said his Mum. "That's your big clever brother."

Charlie sat down and played with his brother. He was even warmer and cuddlier than the bear.

That night, when Charlie went to bed, he thought of telling the bear all about his baby brother. But he wasn't very surprised to find that the bear was nowhere to be seen, and there were big black paw prints on the window sill.

The Horrible Hat

"*Please*," begged Little Bear, "don't wear that hat."
It was Parents' Day at Little Bear's school, and his mother was getting ready to set off.

"Don't be silly, Little Bear," she said, picking up the big purple and orange hat. "It's a beautiful hat."

Little Bear hid his face in his paws. His mother did her best to embarrass him on every occasion. Probably nobody else's mother would be wearing a hat *at all*.

Little Bear followed his mother miserably to the car. Dangling feathers tickled his nose all the way to the school.

When Mrs. Bear got out of the car at the school, everybody turned to look at her. Little Bear wished he was even smaller. He wanted to curl up and never see any of his friends again. But his mother was striding toward the school, calling and waving.

Little Bear did the only thing he could. He hurried off to hide in the coat room.

In another room, Old Boffin Bear was showing an experiment to some parents when something went horribly wrong. There was a burst of orange flame and the next minute little flames were dancing along the desk.

"Fire!" yelled Old Boffin Bear. "Everybody out! Follow me!"

Outside everybody was present and correct ... except one.

"Where's Little Bear?" cried Little Bear's mother. "I'm going back in!"

The rooms were filled with smoke, but she found a little gap of clear air near the floor. So she crawled on her paws and knees.

Little Bear crouched in
the cloakroom. Then he
thought he saw something
moving through the smoke. It
was round and orange and it had
purple dangly bits all round. Little
Bear had never been so pleased
to see that hat!

When Little Bear and
his mother appeared in
the playground, everyone
clapped and cheered.

"Oh dear," said
Little Bear's teacher.
"Look at your beautiful
hat, Mrs Bear." It was
true. The hat was
blackened by smoke and
the edges were drooping.

"Don't worry," said Little Bear,
giving her a big hug. "I'm going to
save up and buy you an even *bigger*
hat. Just you wait and see."

The Most Beautiful Bear

"I am the most beautiful teddy bear in the world," thought Mopsybell. Her fur was fluffy. Her paws were pink . Her eyes were bright and shiny. She was sure that the next little girl to come into the shop would want her.

"She'll love me and look after me and keep me safe and warm," thought Mopsybell. "And I'll live in the kind of house that is just right for a beautiful bear like me."

Just then a little girl *did* come into the shop with her grandmother.

"Now Juliette," said Grandma. "You may choose any teddy bear."

The little girl scowled.

"I don't like bears," she said. "They're for babies. I'd much rather have a robot."

"Don't be silly, dear," said Grandma. "What about that big beautiful bear in the window?"

Mopsybell wriggled on her shelf. She was going to be chosen! But the little girl groaned.

"That's the most stupid-looking bear I've ever seen," she said.

Mopsybell was so shocked, she nearly fell off the shelf. What a *horrible* child!

Juliette was looking at a model dinosaur with huge teeth. "I'd rather have this," she said. "It reminds me of *you*, Grandma."

But Grandma was firm. "I know you'll love this bear, dear," she said.

"I am still the most beautiful bear," thought Mopsybell as they went home. "Juliette will know that as soon as she has a good look at me."

Sure enough, when Grandma had taken Juliette home and hurried off to catch her train, the little girl took a long hard look at her bear.

"I *can* think of some uses for you," she said.

All too soon, Mopsybell found out what she had meant. Mopsybell was just the right size for Juliette's parachute experiments. Tied to a pillow case, she was dropped out of all the upstairs windows.

Then Juliette decided to grow things instead. She tied Mopsybell to a stake as a bear scarecrow, to keep birds away from her seeds!

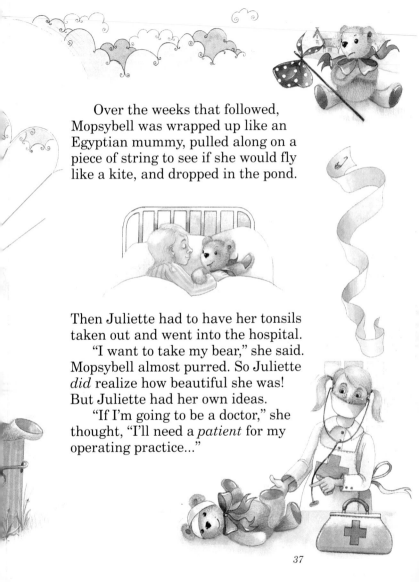

Over the weeks that followed, Mopsybell was wrapped up like an Egyptian mummy, pulled along on a piece of string to see if she would fly like a kite, and dropped in the pond.

Then Juliette had to have her tonsils taken out and went into the hospital.

"I want to take my bear," she said. Mopsybell almost purred. So Juliette *did* realize how beautiful she was! But Juliette had her own ideas.

"If I'm going to be a doctor," she thought, "I'll need a *patient* for my operating practice..."

Mr. Bear's New House

Da, da, dum, dum. "I've never heard such a dreadful noise," groaned Mr. Bear. His neighbour was playing his drums again. "There's only one answer," thought Mr. Bear. "I'm going to have to move."

The next morning, Mr. Bear set out to find another house. The first one he looked at seemed perfect. Mr. Bear was about to say, "I'll take it!" when the house began a strange sort of shivering and shaking.

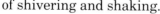

"It's an earthquake!" cried Mr. Bear.

"Did I mention that the train station is very convenient?" asked the agent who was showing Mr. Bear round.

"*Too* convenient," said Mr. Bear.

The next house seemed much better. There were no trains for miles around. Mr. Bear opened his mouth to say that he would like to move in, but his words were drowned out by a screaming, roaring, rushing overhead.

"Sorry," said the agent, "I didn't hear you. Planes do low-flying exercises over this hill."

"This is no good for me," said Mr. Bear firmly. "Isn't there anywhere that is far away from trains or planes or any kind of noise?"

"It's funny you should say that," said the agent. "I've got just the place."

Half an hour later, Mr. Bear was in a boat being rowed toward a lighthouse. Mr. Bear explored it.

"I like it very much," he said. "But what is that noise?"

40

"What noise?" asked the agent.

"*That* noise," said Mr. Bear. "A coming-and-going wooshing noise."

"I can't hear anything," said the agent. "Except the sea, of course."

"Ah," said Mr. Bear. He thanked the agent and went home. When the drumming nextdoor began again, Mr. Bear just smiled. "I do believe he's improving," he said.

The Exciting Life of Uncle Bobo

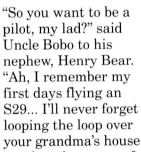

"So you want to be a pilot, my lad?" said Uncle Bobo to his nephew, Henry Bear. "Ah, I remember my first days flying an S29... I'll never forget looping the loop over your grandma's house one day. I was so low that some of her laundry got caught on the tail and I flew back to base with grandpa's underpants flying out behind!"

"Gosh," said Henry. Maybe he wouldn't be a pilot. It would be better to do something that no one in the family had ever done before.

"I've decided to be chef," he said.

"Ah, a chef?" said Uncle Bobo, when next he visited. "Did I tell you about the time I was chef to Prince Bruinski? I remember when the King of Oursania fell into one of my giant cakes. It took them three days to find him. How we all laughed!"

"Goodness," said Henry. Perhaps he wouldn't be a chef after all. That day he saw an interesting word in the dictionary. "I'm going to be an ent-o-mol-o-gist," he told his family. "It's someone who studies insects."

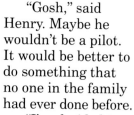

43

A few days later there was a postcard from Uncle Bobo. On the front was a picture of a tropical forest. Henry read the card with a sinking feeling in his tummy. "Dear Henry," it said. "Greetings from my entomological tour of Brazil. This morning I discovered three species of giant ant previously unknown to bear. Best wishes, Uncle Bobo."

Henry sighed. There must be *something* that Uncle Bobo wasn't an expert at. He thought long and hard. By the time Uncle Bobo came to his birthday party, he had decided.

"When I grow up," he said, "I'll be the most famous Henry in the world."

But Uncle Bobo didn't hesitate.

"Goodness me," he said. "It seems only yesterday that I changed my name from Henry to Bobo."

Henry almost cried.

"Don't tease Henry, Bobo," said Aunt Hilda. "You've only had one job in your life. Tell him what you do."

"Can't you guess?" asked Uncle Bobo. "I make up stories for children. And they could be about anything you can think of ... even myself!"

Henry felt better. "When *I* grow up," he said. "I'm going to be a writer. And I'll have lots to say about *uncles*."

Bears Everywhere

Joseph was the easiest boy in the world to please. He liked *anything* with bears on it. He had bears on his slippers and bears on his socks. His bedroom curtains had bear paw prints all over them. He had lots of stories about bears, and on his bed sat his own special teddy bear, Rufus.

Joe loved Rufus best of all. He told the old bear all his secrets and all his worries. And Rufus seemed to understand.

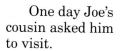

One day Joe's cousin asked him to visit.

"You can help Joe to pack, Katy," Joe's mother told his big sister. "You *would* have been invited too, if you hadn't put gravy in Aunt Sue's purse." Katy grumbled all the time as she helped to pack Joe's clothes.

"Joe, what are you *doing*?" she asked.

"I'm putting Rufus in," said Joe. "He doesn't really like being inside, but he might get lost on the train."

"But you can't take *Rufus*!" laughed Katy. "Everyone will think you're a real baby. Baby Joe, Baby Joe, has to take his teddy bear!"

Joe put Rufus back on the bed. He felt a cold space in his tummy.

Later on, in the train with Aunt Susan, he almost forgot about Rufus. And it was exciting seeing the farm and the animals.

But Joe was very quiet as they had supper. Later, he lay very still in the strange bedroom opposite his cousin's. There were roses on the wallpaper. In the dark, they looked like ogres' faces.

"Oh Rufus," said Joe, "I wish you were here."

During the day, Joe almost forgot that he was sad. But at night he couldn't sleep. Aunt Susan was worried.

"He won't tell *me* what's the matter," she said to her husband.

"Why don't you try?"

Uncle Richard sat on Joe's bed.

"You know," he said. "When I used to stay with my Granny, I never felt homesick because I took my old bear, Mr. Bumble, with me. He was my best friend." Then Joe told Uncle Richard all about Rufus and how he missed him. Uncle Richard smiled.

"I guess I could get along without Mr. Bumble for a night or two, if you'd like to borrow him."

Joe opened his eyes wide.

"But you're older than *me*!" he said.

"Just a bit," grinned his uncle. "What has someone been saying to you? Just between you and me, Joe, I feel rather sorry for people who don't understand about teddy bears, don't you?"

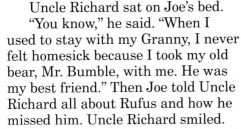

Grandfather Bear Goes Fishing

"I'll be back this evening, dear," said Grandfather Bear to Grandmother Bear. "I'm going to have a nice quiet day fishing down on the river."

"Why you want to go sitting around on drafty riverbanks, I'll never know," grumbled his wife.

"I'll wear my warmest coat, dear," murmured Grandfather Bear, as he left. He was looking forward to a long, peaceful day, sitting on the riverbank.

Grandfather Bear soon found a good place to sit, where passing bears would not disturb him with chatter.

"Peace and quiet at last," said Grandfather Bear. But five minutes later, someone coughed behind him.

"It's only me," said little Bruno Bear, who lived down the road. "Mrs. Bear was worried your ears would get cold. So I've brought your hat." Grandfather Bear couldn't be angry.

"Thank you very much," he said.

Just as Grandfather Bear got settled, he was disturbed again. It was his friend from next door.

"Your wife asked me to bring your scarf," explained the friend. "It *is* rather chilly today."

"Thank you," said Grandfather Bear a little irritably.

Grandfather Bear took a deep breath of country air. All at once, a horrible noise shattered the peace of the riverbank. It was Grandfather Bear's nephew on his motorbike.

"What are you doing?" cried the old bear in dismay.

"Sorry," said his nephew. "But Aunty was sure you would need a hot snack. I brought it as fast as I could so that it wouldn't get cold."

Grandfather Bear sighed. Come to think of it, he did feel a little bit empty somewhere behind his third waistcoat button.

When he had eaten his snack, Grandfather Bear felt full and warm and happy. He settled down for a little snooze after his snack.

Seconds later he heard a voice.

"Mr. Bear! Are you all right?" It was Maisie from the Post Office.

"Mrs. Bear knows that I always take a walk along the river at lunchtime," she said. "She asked me to bring you this flask of coffee."

"Thank you," said Grandfather Bear weakly. Tired and contented, he decided it was time to pack up.

"I'm home, dear," called the old bear, as he walked into the hallway. Grandmother Bear hurried to meet him. "Did you catch anything?"

Grandfather Bear raised his eyes to the ceiling. "No dear," he smiled. "Not even a cold!"

Harold Hubertus Bear

Harold Hubertus Bear, HH to his friends, was no ordinary bear. His great grandmother had been a Princess among the royal Russian bears. His mother came from a long line of bears who had rubbed paws with Dukes and Countesses. In fact, he was a very well connected bear indeed.

HH was a kind bear and many people were very fond of him, but he was rather pompous and liked to hear the sound of his own voice. In fact very little happened in Bearport that Harold Hubertus didn't express an opinion about.

"When it comes to matters of importance," he would say. "You need a bear who has seen a bit of life."

"It's high time that bear came back down to earth," said Mr. Bloomer the baker. "Any ideas, Basil?" Basil, his nephew, looked thoughtful.

A few weeks later the whole town was buzzing with news. Princess Ursula Berelli was coming to visit Harold Hubertus.

"She's a rather distant … er … cousin, I think," said Hubertus.

Harold Hubertus worked hard to make sure that the visit would be a success. He had several rooms in the Hall redecorated. He had six extra gardeners working on the lawns and ten extra cooks in the kitchen.

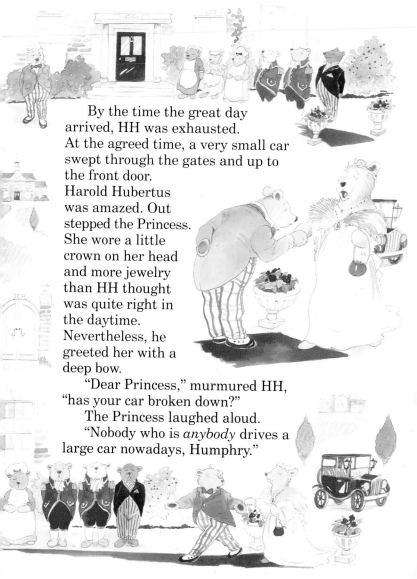

By the time the great day
arrived, HH was exhausted.
At the agreed time, a very small car
swept through the gates and up to
the front door.
Harold Hubertus
was amazed. Out
stepped the Princess.
She wore a little
crown on her head
and more jewelry
than HH thought
was quite right in
the daytime.
Nevertheless, he
greeted her with a
deep bow.

"Dear Princess," murmured HH,
"has your car broken down?"

The Princess laughed aloud.

"Nobody who is *anybody* drives a
large car nowadays, Humphry."

The Princess allowed herself to be led into the dining room, where the tables were piled high.

"Dear Horribilus, I'm afraid I never touch anything richer than a slice of toast. Why not give this food to the people of the town?"

"What a charming idea," said HH with a gulp. "I'll tell the servants to take it away at once."

"Tell me, Hardboiledus," cried the Princess, "are you really so behind the times as to have servants? I can hardly believe it."

"Er ... that sort of thing is no longer done, I suppose, in your circle?" enquired HH in a shaky voice.

"Goodness me no, Hurglegurglus," laughed the Princess. "I will help you to take all this delicious food to the good townspeople!"

It was not until he was waving her goodbye, that HH noticed that the Princess was wearing a bracelet that read, quite clearly, *Basil*.

"I fear," he said to himself, "that I have been a very foolish old bear. But everyone else is happy and that makes me happy too. And only a bear with real pedigree can take a joke as well as I can, after all."

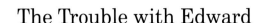

The Trouble with Edward

"Where's that bear?" roared Mr. Teddington from the garage. "Someone – and I think I know who – has filled my boots with mud!"

Edward tried to explain.

"I was trying to start a wormery, dad. We've been learning about worms at school."

"Come here at once and clean out these boots!" replied his father.

It didn't seem to matter what he did, Edward was always in trouble. Even if he was trying to do something helpful, it always seemed to go wrong.

Later that day, when she had finished cleaning up after Edward, Mrs. Teddington flopped into a chair.

"What *are* we going to do with that bear?"

"I think the problem is that he doesn't have an older bear to look up to and copy. I thought we could invite your friend Violet and her boy Billy to stay with us," said her husband.

"*Two* boys in the house?" Mrs. Teddington shuddered. But she remembered Billy handing out hymn books very quietly at her sister's wedding and reluctantly agreed.

As soon as Billy arrived in the house, Mr. and Mrs. Teddington felt that they had done the right thing. Billy was clean and polite, but more important, he was *thoughtful*.

Billy polished Mr. Teddington's car so that you could see your face in it. *And* he saved the rinsing water for Mrs. Teddington's potted plants.

"He's having a very good effect on Edward," whispered Mrs. Teddington to her husband. "Although sometimes I think he is just a little bit *too* good."

On Billy's last day, the whole family went for a picnic by the river.

"We're a little too near the river for safety," said Billy. "One false step could cause a dangerous situation."

"Oh nonsense," cried Mr. T. "It's perfectly safe." But as he spoke, he slipped. SPLASH!

"He can't swim!" yelled Mrs. Teddington. "Somebody do *something!*"

"Dad!" cried Edward. "I'll save you!" and he plunged into the water.

"I shall stay safely away from the edge," said Billy calmly. "People are often drowned trying to save someone."

But Mr. Teddington climbed out of the river with a broad smile.

"In case you hadn't noticed, Billy," he said, "the water only came up to my knees. I *know* accidents can happen even in shallow water, but Edward is a very good swimmer and there are things that are more important than being sensible. I'm very proud of Edward."

Mrs. T. gave them both a big hug. "There wasn't any need to worry," smiled Mr. Teddington.

"I wasn't really worried," said his wife. "Especially now I can see *exactly* where Edward gets his ... Edwardness from!"

A Bear at Bedtime

One bear in a bed is cuddly, and two are better still. With three teddy bears, you are sure to be warm, and just one more is no problem at all.

Five teddy bears in a bed can help you sleep, while six teddy bears are very good indeed. Seven is a lucky number for bears. And eight teddy bears are best of all.

But nine teddy bears in a bed? Be careful! There may not be room for you...

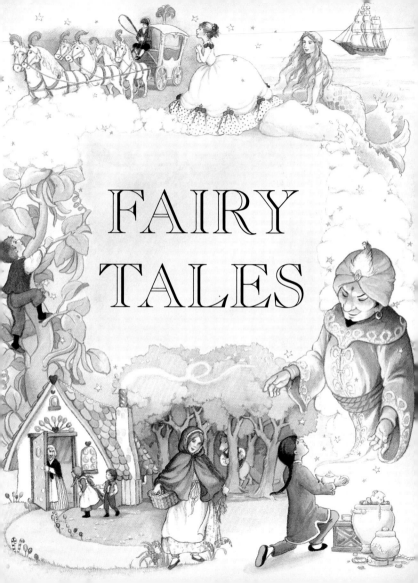

FAIRY
TALES

Little Red Riding Hood

Once upon a time there was a little girl who had a red cloak that she loved to wear. Because of this, everyone called her Little Red Riding Hood.

One morning, Little Red Riding Hood's mother received a letter.

"It's from Granny," she said. "She's not feeling very well. You can go to see her, Little Red Riding Hood, but remember not to wander from the path or talk to anyone on the way."

So Little Red Riding Hood set off for her Granny's cottage in the woods.

It was a lovely day. Soon Little Red Riding Hood saw some pretty flowers growing beneath the trees. As she stopped to pick some, a large wolf stepped out from behind a nearby tree.

"Good afternoon, my dear," he said. "What lovely flowers."

"I'm sorry," said the little girl firmly. "But I'm not allowed to talk to strangers. I'm on my way to see my Granny and I mustn't be late."

Half an hour later, Little Red
Riding Hood arrived at her Granny's
cottage. The door was open, so Little
Red Riding Hood walked in and
tiptoed over to the bed. Granny
really didn't look very well at all.

"Granny!" cried Little Red Riding
Hood. "What big ears you have!"

"The better to hear you with, my
dear," said Granny.

Little Red Riding Hood looked a
little closer.

"Why, Granny!" she said. "What
big eyes you have!"

"The better to see you with, my
dear," whispered Granny.

But Little Red Riding Hood had seen something very odd indeed.

"Why, Granny!" she gasped. "What big teeth you have!"

"The better to eat you with!" shouted the wolf, leaping out of the bed! Luckily, a woodman who was working nearby heard the little girl's scream and hurried in with his axe. The wolf ran off into the trees.

Little Red Riding Hood soon found where her Granny had hidden and gave her a hug.

"I feel much better now!" said Granny.

The Little Mermaid

Long ago and far away, the King of the mer-people ruled all the lands under the sea. He had six beautiful mermaid daughters, who loved to play in the clear blue water. But they were not allowed to rise to the surface and look at the world where human beings lived.

"You are all much too young to leave the sea," said their grandmother. "But I will tell you strange tales of the world of human beings if you are very good."

As the Princesses grew up, they each swam up to view the outside world. At last it was the turn of the youngest Princess.

Above the waves, the sky was dark. As a great storm blew up, a ship was driven upon rocks near the shore and a young man was thrown into the water. The little mermaid brought him safely to shore, leaving him on a sandy beach.

The little mermaid hid and waited. Soon some girls came along the beach and found the young man.

"It's the Prince!" they cried.

"Where is the lovely girl who saved me?" he asked. But no one knew.

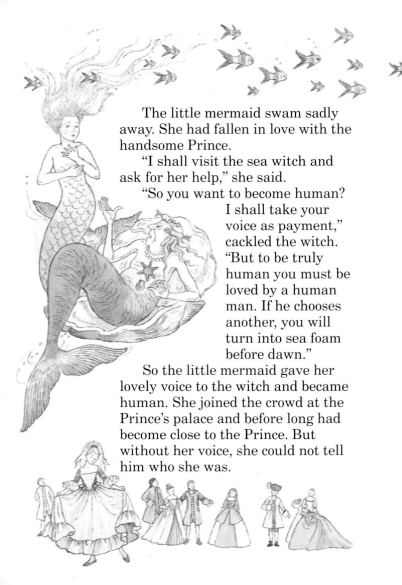

The little mermaid swam sadly away. She had fallen in love with the handsome Prince.

"I shall visit the sea witch and ask for her help," she said.

"So you want to become human? I shall take your voice as payment," cackled the witch. "But to be truly human you must be loved by a human man. If he chooses another, you will turn into sea foam before dawn."

So the little mermaid gave her lovely voice to the witch and became human. She joined the crowd at the Prince's palace and before long had become close to the Prince. But without her voice, she could not tell him who she was.

One day the Prince said, "We are sailing to meet a beautiful Princess. I may marry her." The little mermaid thought that her heart would break.

When the Prince met the lovely Princess, he was dazzled by her beauty. The wedding was planned to take place the next day.

The little mermaid wept.

"You can save yourself," cried her sisters from the sea, "if you kill the Prince!"

But the little mermaid loved him too much to do so and threw herself into the sea. But she did not turn into foam. She became a spirit of the air and was happy at last.

Cinderella

Poor Cinderella! All day long her two sisters yelled and scolded and made her do all the work. Although she had no fine jewels or pretty shoes, she was far more beautiful than they were, which made them dislike her even more.

One day a messenger from the palace invited all the young ladies from near and far to a ball to celebrate the Prince's birthday.

"Perhaps he will choose a bride at the ball!" said the sisters. They did not think of taking Cinderella.

After her sisters had left, Cinderella sat in front of the dying fire. "I wish that I could go to the ball," she sighed. Suddenly an old woman stood before her.

"I am your fairy godmother, Cinderella," she said. "And you *shall* go to the ball."

The fairy asked Cinderella to bring her a pumpkin. With a wave of her wand, she turned it into a beautiful golden coach. Then she turned six mice into six white horses to pull the coach. Finally, she waved her wand again and gave Cinderella a beautiful dress. "Now you are ready for the ball, my dear," she smiled.

"But remember, the magic only lasts until midnight. Before the clock strikes, you must hurry home," warned the fairy.

When Cinderella arrived at the ball in her golden coach, everyone in wondered who the beautiful stranger could be. The Prince himself led her to the ballroom and would let no one else dance with her all evening.

But as she whirled around the floor, Cinderella suddenly heard the great clock on the tower outside begin to strike. It was midnight!

"I'm sorry," she whispered and fled, leaving behind a glass slipper.

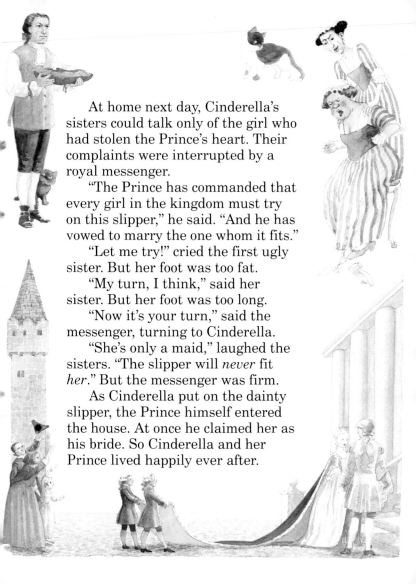

At home next day, Cinderella's sisters could talk only of the girl who had stolen the Prince's heart. Their complaints were interrupted by a royal messenger.

"The Prince has commanded that every girl in the kingdom must try on this slipper," he said. "And he has vowed to marry the one whom it fits."

"Let me try!" cried the first ugly sister. But her foot was too fat.

"My turn, I think," said her sister. But her foot was too long.

"Now it's your turn," said the messenger, turning to Cinderella.

"She's only a maid," laughed the sisters. "The slipper will *never* fit *her*." But the messenger was firm.

As Cinderella put on the dainty slipper, the Prince himself entered the house. At once he claimed her as his bride. So Cinderella and her Prince lived happily ever after.

Snow White and the Seven Dwarfs

One winter's day, a Queen sat sewing. "I wish that my daughter could have skin as white as snow, lips as red as blood and hair as black as this window frame," she sighed. Soon she gave birth to a daughter, just as she had described, and named her Snow White.

Sadly, the Queen died soon after, and the King remarried. His bride was a very beautiful woman, but her heart was cold. Every day she looked into a magic mirror and asked,
*"Mirror, mirror, on the wall,
Who is the fairest one of all?"*

The mirror always replied,
"Many are lovely beyond compare,
But you are the fairest of the fair."
At last the day came when the mirror gave a new reply,
"Though you are lovely I declare,
Snow White is the fairest of the fair."
The Queen was furious. She told a huntsman to take the girl to the forest and kill her.

The huntsman was not a cruel man, so he led Snow White into the thickest part of the forest and left her.
Snow White was terrified. She stumbled through the trees until she saw a little house. Worn out with fear and hunger, she crept inside and fell asleep. When she awoke, seven little men were looking down at her. They explained that they lived there.
"You can stay with us," they said.

So Snow White looked after the dwarfs and their little house. One day an old woman knocked on the door.

"Try this special apple, my dear," she said. Snow White did not known that she was the wicked Queen in disguise.

Poor Snow White took just one bite of the apple. It was poisoned! When the dwarfs came home, all their loving care could not revive her.

"This is the Queen's work," they said angrily.

The dwarfs could not bear to bury Snow White, so they put her in a glass coffin in a clearing of the forest and kept watch beside her.

One day a Prince came riding by. The moment he saw Snow White, he fell in love with her.

"Though she can never be my bride," he said to the dwarfs, "let me take her back to my palace."

Sadly, the dwarfs agreed, but as they helped to move her, the piece of apple that had caught in Snow White's throat was dislodged and she woke up. As soon as she saw the Prince, she loved him and soon became his wife. The evil Queen left in a fury and was never seen again.

Thumbelina

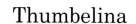

Once there was a woman who longed to have a little girl of her own. She went to a wise woman and asked for her help.

"Take this seed," said the old woman, "and plant it. You will see your wish come true." So the woman did as she was told. The seed grew into a plant with a yellow flower. In the middle of the flower was a little girl, no bigger than a thumb. So the woman called her Thumbelina.

The woman took good care of
Thumbelina, but one day, a mother
toad hopped in through the window
and carried the little girl away.

"You are so beautiful," croaked
the toad to the frightened little girl.
"You shall be married to my son."
And she left Thumbelina on a lily
leaf in the middle of the river.

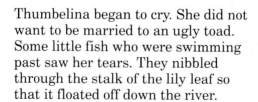

Thumbelina began to cry. She did not
want to be married to an ugly toad.
Some little fish who were swimming
past saw her tears. They nibbled
through the stalk of the lily leaf so
that it floated off down the river.

All summer long Thumbelina
was happy, but when winter came,
she grew cold and hungry. One day,
Thumbelina met a fieldmouse coming
out of her house. "You can stay with
me for a little while," said the mouse.

"You must meet my friend the
mole," the mouse went on. "He is
looking for a wife."
So Thumbelina
went to see him.
His house was
dark and cold and
something was
lying on the floor.

"It's a dead bird," said the mole, but Thumbelina bent down and felt the bird's body. Its heart was beating!

"I will look after you," whispered Thumbelina. She cared for the bird until he was well enough to fly away.

In the spring, Thumbelina sat sadly looking at the blue sky. It was time for her to marry the mole. Suddenly she saw a bird high above. It was her swallow!

"Climb onto my back," he said, "and come with me."

After flying across land and sea, the swallow landed in a flowery meadow. As Thumbelina looked around, she saw little flower people – just like her!

"Welcome to our land," they said. "We will call you Maia." Thumbelina had found her real home at last.

Rumpelstiltskin

Once there was a silly man who had a very beautiful daughter. He boasted to the King that she could spin straw into gold! The King smiled. "If she can, I will marry her!" he said.

So the poor girl was brought to the palace and shut into a room with some straw and a spinning wheel.

"You have until morning to spin that straw into gold," said the King. "But if you fail, you must die."

As the door clanged shut, the girl burst into tears. Then, in a puff of smoke, a little man appeared.

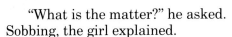

"What is the matter?" he asked.
Sobbing, the girl explained.

"But that's easily solved,"
laughed the strange little man. "You
give me ... let's see ... your gold ring,
and I'll spin this straw into gold."

The poor girl was only too glad
to make the exchange. Long before
morning, the little man had done
as he promised and disappeared.

The King was delighted
when he saw the golden
thread and at once
he wanted more.

"Twice more, and we will be sure
that this was not a trick," he said.

On the next night, the little man
spun the straw in return for the girl's
glass beads, but on the third night,
she had nothing left to give him.

"When you are Queen," he said,
"you can give me your firstborn child."

This seemed so unlikely that the girl agreed and the little man worked as before.

The next day, when he saw all the golden thread, the King kept his promise to marry the girl. She was very happy, especially when she had a baby daughter.

One night, the young Queen was startled to see the little man again.

"I've come for your child," he said.

The terrified Queen begged him to take her jewels instead.

"No," said the little man, "but if you guess my name within three days, I will go away and never return.

On the next two nights, the Queen guessed every name she could think of. But the little man shook his head.

On the third day, a soldier told her a strange story. "In the forest," he said, "I heard a little man singing,

'The Queen will never win my game,
For Rumpelstiltskin is my name!' "

That night, the Queen tried again.
"Is your name ... Trip Trap ... or Humpelby Bumpelby?"
"No! No!"
"Then is it ... Rumpelstiltskin?"
The little man stamped his feet so hard that he fell through the floor and was never seen again. The Queen lived happily ever after.

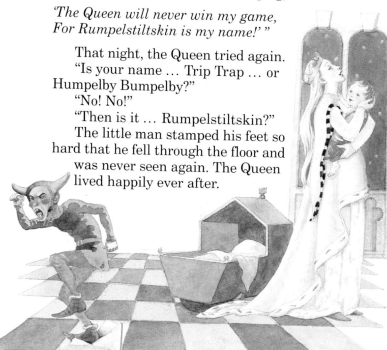

Hansel and Gretel

Once upon a time there was a poor woodcutter who had two children called Hansel and Gretel. Their mother had died when they were small, and the woodcutter's new wife was not used to being so poor.

One evening, as the two hungry children tried to get to sleep, they heard their father and stepmother talking in the next room.

"We cannot afford to feed ourselves *and* the children," said the woman. "At this rate, we shall *all* starve. Tomorrow we must take them into the forest and leave them there."

The woodcutter protested, but he could not bear to lose his wife, and in the end he agreed.

The children were very afraid,
but Hansel comforted his sister.

"Don't worry," he said. "I'll drop
some crumbs along the path, so that
we'll be able to find our way home."

But the next day, when the
children were left in the forest, a
little bird ate up all the crumbs.

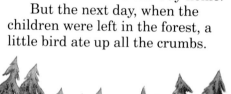

Hungry and afraid, the children
stumbled through the trees. All at
once they saw a house made of candy
and gingerbread! The hungry children
ran toward it and began to eat.

"Eat away!" cackled a voice. It was
a witch who liked to eat children!

At first the witch pretended to be kind, but the next morning she locked Hansel in a shed and forced Gretel to work night and day cooking food for him.

"Soon he'll be fat enough for me to eat," chuckled the witch.

At last the day came when the witch could wait no longer. She ordered Gretel to stoke up the fire under the oven.

"Just poke your head in and see if it is hot enough yet," she said. But Gretel pretended not to understand. Angrily, the old woman pushed her aside. In a flash, the little girl gave the witch a big push and slammed the oven door shut.

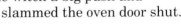

Gretel ran to set her brother free.

"But we are still lost," said Hansel. Then a bird flying high above called to them.

"I ate your crumbs before," it sang. "I will lead you home."

So Hansel and Gretel saw their father again at last. He wept with joy to see them.

"We have one more surprise," smiled the children, emptying their pockets. "With this gold from the witch's house, we shall never be poor again!"

Rapunzel

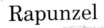

A long time ago there lived a woman who longed for a baby of her own. She wanted this so much that she became ill.

One day the woman looked out of her window and saw some lettuce growing in the garden next door.

"I feel as though I shall die if I don't eat some of that lettuce," she said to her husband.

Now a witch lived in the house next door, but the man loved his wife, so that night he crept over the wall of the garden.

"Do you dare to steal from *me*?" hissed a voice.

It was the witch! The poor man was terrified.

"I'll let you go," said the witch, "if you give me your first child."

The man agreed, thinking that he would have no children, but a few months later, his wife did give birth to a baby girl. True to his promise, the man took her to the witch.

The witch took good care of the little girl, calling her Rapunzel. As she grew older, Rapunzel became very beautiful, so the jealous witch locked her up in a high tower.

When the witch wanted to visit Rapunzel, she would call out, "Rapunzel, Rapunzel, let down your hair." The girl would lower her thick braided hair from the window, and the witch would climb up it.

One day, a Prince rode through the forest. Hidden among the trees, he watched what happened and waited until the witch was gone. Then he went to the bottom of the tower and called, "Rapunzel, Rapunzel, let down your hair." Rapunzel did as she was asked. She was very astonished to see the young man climbing into the room.

Rapunzel and the Prince soon fell in love. All went well until Rapunzel by mistake told the witch of her visitor. In a fury, the witch cut off the girl's hair and sent her to a desert far away. When the Prince arrived, the witch lowered the cut hair from the window, then made him fall into the brambles below.

The Prince was not killed, but his eyes were made blind by the thorns. For years he wandered in search of Rapunzel. At last, one day, he found her. As she clung to him, her tears of joy healed his eyes. Together, they returned to the Prince's kingdom and lived happily ever after.

Jack and the Beanstalk

"We shall have to sell our cow," said Jack's mother. "We have no more money."

So Jack set off to market with the cow, but on the way he met a stranger.

"Why walk all the way to market?" asked the man. "I'll take the cow now and I'll give you these magic beans in return."

Jack was delighted to have a handful of magic beans, but his mother was not so happy. She threw them out of the window. The next morning, a huge bean plant had grown beside the house.

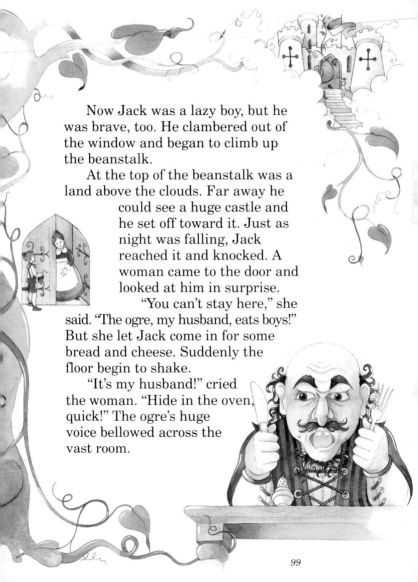

Now Jack was a lazy boy, but he was brave, too. He clambered out of the window and began to climb up the beanstalk.

At the top of the beanstalk was a land above the clouds. Far away he could see a huge castle and he set off toward it. Just as night was falling, Jack reached it and knocked. A woman came to the door and looked at him in surprise.

"You can't stay here," she said. "The ogre, my husband, eats boys!" But she let Jack come in for some bread and cheese. Suddenly the floor begin to shake.

"It's my husband!" cried the woman. "Hide in the oven, quick!" The ogre's huge voice bellowed across the vast room.

"Fee, fie, fo, fum,
I smell the blood
Of an Englishman.
Be he alive,
Or be he dead,
I'll grind his bones
To make my bread."

"That's just the soup
ready for your supper,"
said his wife. Then the ogre shouted,
"Bring me my hen!" His wife went
out and fetched a white hen.

The ogre took the hen and cried,
"Lay!" To Jack's amazement, the hen
laid a golden egg! Again and again,
the ogre ordered the hen to lay, until
there were twelve golden eggs on the
table. Then he fell asleep.

When he heard the ogre snoring,
Jack jumped out of the oven, picked
up the magic hen, and ran away.

He scrambled down the beanstalk, calling out, "Mother! Bring the axe!"

As soon as he was on the ground, Jack cut through the beanstalk with a mighty blow, and the ogre, who had been chasing him, fell to his death.

"Why Jack!" cried his mother. "That is the hen that the wicked ogre stole from your poor father. Now our troubles are over! I will never call you a lazy boy again, for you have saved us all."

So Jack and his mother lived happily ever after, and no more magic beans were ever grown in *their* garden!

The Gingerbread Man

Once upon a time a little old man and a little old woman lived in the country. One day, the little old woman made some ginger cookies. She had some dough left over, so she made a little gingerbread man, with three buttons and two eyes made of raisins and a smiley mouth made out of a cherry. But when the little old woman went to take him out of the oven, the gingerbread man jumped from the tray and ran right out of the door!

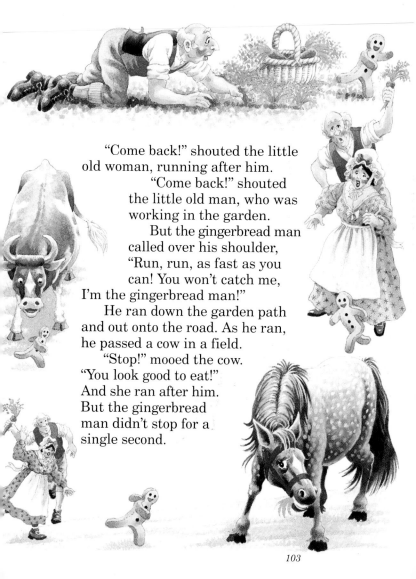

"Come back!" shouted the little old woman, running after him.

"Come back!" shouted the little old man, who was working in the garden.

But the gingerbread man called over his shoulder, "Run, run, as fast as you can! You won't catch me, I'm the gingerbread man!"

He ran down the garden path and out onto the road. As he ran, he passed a cow in a field.

"Stop!" mooed the cow. "You look good to eat!" And she ran after him. But the gingerbread man didn't stop for a single second.

"A little old woman and a little old man couldn't catch me and neither will you! Run, run, as fast as you can! You won't catch me, I'm the gingerbread man!"

In the next field he passed a horse. "Stop!" neighed the horse. "You look good to eat!" But the gingerbread man kept running. It was the same when he passed a rooster on a gate and a pig in a yard. The gingerbread man did not stop for anything ... until he came to a fast-flowing river.

"I can't swim," cried the gingerbread man. "What can I do?"

"Can I help you?" asked a quiet voice. It was a big red fox. "Jump on my back and I will carry you across."

The gingerbread man did as the fox said, and the fox swam into the river.

But soon the fox spoke again. "The water is deeper here. Climb onto my head and you will stay dry." The little man did so.

"The water is even deeper now," said the fox soon. "Climb onto my nose and you'll stay dry."

As soon as the gingerbread man did so, the fox tossed him into the air. The little man fell right into the fox's open mouth. When the little old man and woman came puffing along, only a few crumbs were floating in the water.

Sleeping Beauty

Long ago a King and Queen gave a party to celebrate the birth of their daughter. The proud parents invited all the most important people in the kingdom, including twelve fairies. All the guests brought presents for the baby Princess, but the most valuable gifts of all came from the fairies. One by one they stood over her cradle and smiled down at her.

"I will give her beauty," said one fairy.

"I will give her a loving nature," said the second fairy.

And so it went on, as eleven of the fairies gave their gifts. Suddenly a rush of cold air blew through the room. In the doorway stood a very old woman. She was the thirteenth fairy, who had been totally forgotten.

The thirteenth fairy walked toward the cradle. "On the day that the Princess is eighteen years old, she will prick her finger on a spindle and die," she announced.

In the silence, the twelfth fairy stepped forward. "I cannot undo my sister's words," she said, "but I can soften them. The Princess *will* prick her finger, but instead of dying, she will fall sleep for a hundred years."

While the Princess was still a baby, the King and Queen had all the spindles in the kingdom collected and burned. As everyone had wished, the Princess grew up to be kind, happy and beautiful.

On the morning of her eighteenth birthday, the Princess awoke early and walked in the courtyard of the palace. Suddenly she noticed a little door in a tower that she had never seen before. She opened the door and climbed the winding staircase inside. In a little room at the top, an old woman sat spinning.

Of course, the Princess had never seen such a thing before. She went in and curiously touched the spindle.

As she did so, she
pricked her finger and fell
at once into a deep sleep.
Not only did the Princess
sleep, but the whole castle
stopped just at that moment.

Years passed, and a great hedge
of briars grew up around the palace.
One day a young Prince rode by.
When he heard the story about the
Princess, he was eager to explore.

When the Prince came to the
tower where the Princess lay, he
could not resist bending to kiss her.

The Prince's kiss broke the
fairy's spell. As the Princess
awoke, the whole palace came
back to life. And in the little
tower room, the Princess had
eyes only for the young man
leaning over her, and knew
that she would be his bride.

The Emperor's New Clothes

Once upon a time there was an Emperor who was very vain. All his life, his courtiers had been telling him how wonderful he was. It was not surprising that he had begun to believe it himself.

One day, the Emperor decided that he would like a new suit of clothes. It so happened that in the court at that time there were two wicked men. They told the Emperor that they could make him a suit that was unlike anything that had ever been made before.

"It is made of a new material," said one, "so fine that only the truly intelligent can see it."

This sounded just what the Emperor was looking for. He asked them to begin at once. And so the performance began. The two tailors were given a room in the palace in which to work and every day they asked for more money to buy the thread and cloth they needed. In fact, they did not buy anything at all, but kept the money for themselves.

At last the day came for the first fitting of the suit. The two wicked men pretended to hold something up before the Emperor. "Isn't it lovely?" they gushed. "We are particularly pleased with the button holes. Can you see?"

The Emperor hesitated. He could see nothing at all. But he did not want to appear stupid.

"It is quite beyond words," he said slowly. "I can't find expressions to do it justice. I can truthfully say that I've never seen anything like it."

Then the tailors pretended to try the suit on the Emperor. He was wearing nothing at all!

After several fittings, the suit was announced to be finished. The Emperor was to appear that day in a Grand Parade through the city.

The city streets were full as the Emperor appeared. There was a small silence. No one wanted to appear stupid.

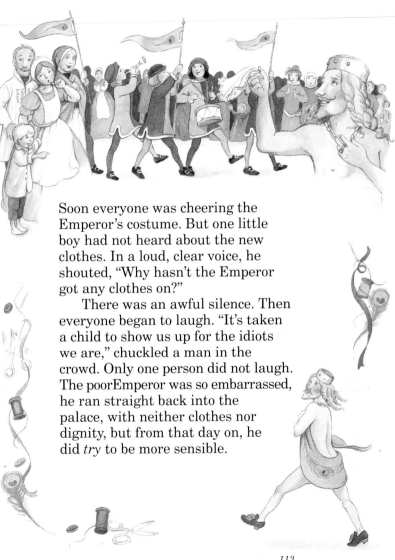

Soon everyone was cheering the Emperor's costume. But one little boy had not heard about the new clothes. In a loud, clear voice, he shouted, "Why hasn't the Emperor got any clothes on?"

There was an awful silence. Then everyone began to laugh. "It's taken a child to show us up for the idiots we are," chuckled a man in the crowd. Only one person did not laugh. The poorEmperor was so embarrassed, he ran straight back into the palace, with neither clothes nor dignity, but from that day on, he did *try* to be more sensible.

The Fisherman and His Wife

There was once a poor fisherman who lived with his wife in a hut near the shore. The hut was a shambles and not very clean.

One day the fisherman went down to the sea and cast his line. Before long he had landed a huge carp. To his astonishment, the fish began to speak.

"Please, throw me back into the sea," it said. "I am not a fish at all but an enchanted Prince."

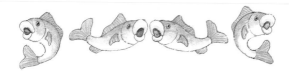

The fisherman was so amazed that he did not know what to say, but threw the fish back as it had asked. When he got home that night, he told his wife what had happened.

"You idiot!" she cried. "You should have asked it to grant a wish. Go back and ask for a pretty cottage instead of this miserable hut."

So the fisherman did as she said. The fish thrashed its tail and the waves frothed and swirled.

"Very well," it said. "Go home. Your wish has been granted."

"Now we want for nothing," sighed the fisherman, when he saw their cottage.

115

But a few weeks later, the fisherman's wife began to complain. "I would much rather live in a castle," she said. Go back and ask that fish."

Reluctantly, the fisherman went back to the shore and explained his wife's wish. The carp splashed angrily in the water. The sky grew dark and the waves crashed onto the beach. "Very well," said the fish. "Go home. Your wish has been granted."

When the fisherman arrived home, he found his wife in gorgeous clothes ordering a whole army of servants around in a huge castle.

"Now our happiness is complete," said the fisherman.

But only a few days later, his wife was complaining again. "I want to be ruler of the world!" she declared.

With a heavy heart, the poor fisherman set off for the seashore. When he told the fish what his wife wanted now, thunder rumbled overhead. Above the crashing of the waves, the fisherman heard the fish.

"Go home. Your wife has what she deserves."

When the man arrived home, he found his wife back in the hut where they had started. And as far as I know, they are still living there to this day.

The Frog Prince

In a land far away, there lived a King who had seven beautiful daughters. But the youngest Princess was the most beautiful and the King loved her best of all.

Unfortunately, she was also very spoiled and used to having her own way. She pleased herself from dawn to dusk.

One day the youngest Princess went into the woods near the royal palace and sat beneath the trees by an old well, where it was cool.

As she sat, she gently
threw a golden ball into
the air and caught it
again. But before she
knew what was happening,
the ball had fallen into the deep well.

The youngest Princess was furious.
She was very fond of the golden ball.

Just then a little voice close to
her ear croaked, "I can help you!"

Only two inches away was a big
green frog. "I could hop into the well
and bring back your ball," he said, "if
you would be my friend."

"Very well," said the Princess.
The frog jumped into the water
and brought out the golden
ball. But the Princess at once
ran off towards the castle,
leaving the frog behind.

That night, as the Princess sat at supper, there was a knock at the door.

"Your Highness," said a servant to the youngest Princess. "It's ... er ... a frog, asking for you."

"Tell him I'm busy," said the Princess quickly. "I can't see him now." But the King asked who was at the door, and reluctantly, the Princess told him the whole story.

"A promise is a promise," said the King, sternly.

Miserably, the Princess picked up the frog.

"Offer our guest some food," said the King. And the Princess did so.

When it was time to go to bed, the Princess took the frog to her room.

"Now lift me onto the pillow," he begged. The Princess could hardly bear it, but she did so. As she placed the frog on her silken pillow, an astonishing thing happened. The frog became a handsome Prince, who sat smiling at her.

"You have saved me from an evil spell," he said, and before long the Prince and Princess were married.

The Princess and the Pea

Once upon a time there was a Prince who wanted to be married. He insisted that he could only marry a real Princess.

One stormy night, the Prince was at home in the royal palace with the King and Queen. Suddenly, a knock was heard at the palace door. There on the doorstep stood a lovely girl, dripping wet and shivering with cold.

"I am a Princess," said the stranger. "Please may I come in until the storm has passed?"

As soon as the Prince saw the girl, he fell head over heels in love.

"We'll soon see if she is a real princess," said the Queen.

When the girl was shown to her room, she saw that the bed was piled high with twenty feather mattresses.

The next morning, the royal family was breakfasting when their guest appeared.

"Did you sleep well?" asked the King.

"No," replied the girl. "A lump in my mattress kept me awake all night."

"Then you *are* a real Princess," said the Queen. "Only a real Princess has such delicate skin that she can feel the tiny pea I placed under the bed."

So the Prince and the Princess were married and lived happily ever after.

The Enormous Turnip

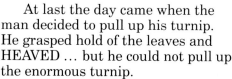

There was once a man who had a vegetable garden that was his pride and joy. One day he planted two rows of turnip seeds. In no time at all the plants were growing strongly. But one plant grew more strongly than all the rest! It grew and it grew, until it was the biggest turnip that anyone had ever seen.

At last the day came when the man decided to pull up his turnip. He grasped hold of the leaves and HEAVED … but he could not pull up the enormous turnip.

So the man called to his wife. "Please come and help me!"

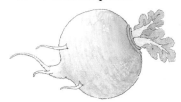

But the man and the wife together could not pull up the enormous turnip.

Just then a little boy walked past. "I'll help!" he said. But the boy and the man and the wife together could not pull up the turnip.

Next the boy's sister joined in. But it was no use.

A dog joined the chain. But the turnip did not move.

A cat pulled as well. But the enormous turnip stayed in the ground.

Finally, a little mouse helped the man and his wife and the boy and the girl and the dog and the cat to pull up the turnip. They heaved and they heaved and ... slowly ... the turnip came out of the ground. Phew! I believe they are eating it still!

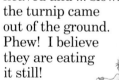

Aladdin

Long ago a boy called Aladdin lived with his mother. They were very poor. One day, as Aladdin walked through the bustling market, he was greeted by a stranger, who held out two golden coins.

"At last I have found you!" cried the stranger. "I am your father's brother."

Aladdin and his mother welcomed the stranger as one of the family. On the third day, he said to Aladdin, "I have seen your eyes sparkle at my stories of faraway places. Come with me and I will show you something strange and wonderful."

Without hesitating, Aladdin followed the visitor out of the city.

In a wooded valley, the visitor lit a fire and threw some magic powder into it. He was not a kindly uncle at all, but a wicked wizard, who needed Aladdin for a special task.

The wizard showed the terrified boy a passageway.

"Go down the steps," he said, "but do not touch the gold and jewels that you see. In the furthest room, you will find an old lamp. Bring that lamp to me. But take this ring. It will protect you."

Aladdin did as he was told, but as he returned, holding the lamp, he heard the wizard plotting to kill him. Aladdin wrung his hands. In doing so, he rubbed the ring that the wizard had given him. All at once, a genie appeared.

"What is your will?" he asked.

"I'd like to go home," stammered Aladdin. At once it was done.

After that, the magic ring and the magic lamp meant that Aladdin and his mother lived very comfortably, but one day Aladdin caught sight of the Emperor's daughter and he fell in love with her.

Once again, he called upon the genie of the lamp to help. Aladdin and his bride were blissfully happy, but the wicked wizard managed to win back the lamp by trickery. With the help of the genie, he flew away to Africa, taking Aladdin's palace and the lovely Princess with him.

The genie of the ring and the Princess's cleverness defeated the wizard, and Aladdin and his wife lived happily ever after.

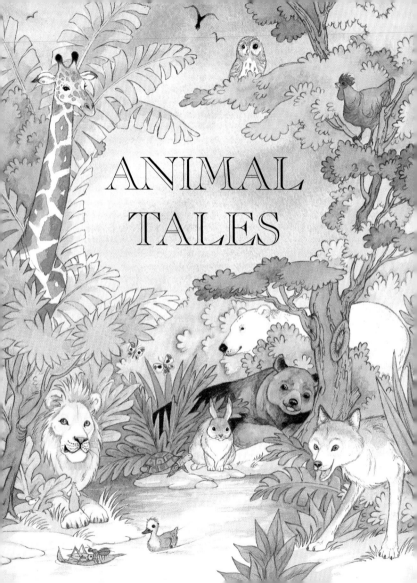

ANIMAL
TALES

The Three Little Pigs

Once there were three little pigs who decided to set off into the wide world to find homes of their own. "Remember," said their mother, "to watch out for the big, bad wolf!" The little pigs did not go far before they stopped to rest. Just then a man passed, carrying a load of straw. "With that straw I could build a strong, safe house," said the first little pig. And so he did.

Meanwhile, the other two little pigs had walked on until they met a farmer with a load of sticks.

"With those sticks I could build a strong, safe house," said the second little pig. And so he did.

Meanwhile, the third little pig had walked even further. Soon he met a workman with a cart piled high with fine red building bricks.

"With those bricks I could build a strong, safe house," said the third little pig. And that is exactly what he did.

That night the first little
pig heard a voice calling.

"Little pig, little pig, let
me come in!" It was the wolf!

"No, no, by the hair of my chinny
chin chin, I'll not let you in!"

"Then I'll huff, and I'll puff, and
I'll blow your house down!"

And the wolf huffed and puffed
and blew the house down. But the
little pig ran quickly to his brother.

The next night the two pigs in
the house of sticks heard a voice.

"Little pigs, little pigs, let me
come in!"

"No, no, by the hair of our chinny
chin chins, we'll not let you in!"

"Then I'll huff, and I'll puff, and I'll blow your house down!"

The wolf huffed and puffed and he blew down the house of sticks, but the two little pigs ran to their brother.

That night the wolf came again.

"Little pigs, little pigs, let me come in!"

"No, no, by the hair of our chinny chin chins, we will not let you in!"

"Then I'll huff, and I'll puff, and I'll blow your house down!" And he huffed and puffed but he could not blow the house down.

The wolf was *cross*. "I'll climb down the chimney!" he said.

But the third little pig put a huge pot of water on the fire. When the wolf leapt down the chimney, he landed with a splash. And that was the end of him!

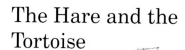

The Hare and the Tortoise

There was once a hare who was very proud of his running. "No one is as speedy as me!" he cried. "Would anyone like to race?"

"No thanks!" laughed the other animals. "We know you can run faster than any of us."

But one little voice piped up politely behind him. "I'll give you a race if you like, Mr. Hare," it said.

The hare turned around in surprise. Standing before him was a wrinkly old tortoise.

"Oh my!" replied the hare. "You make me tremble, *Mr.* Tortoise."

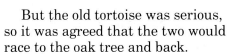

But the old tortoise was serious, so it was agreed that the two would race to the oak tree and back.

"On your marks! Get set! Go!" yelled the squirrel.

In a couple of seconds, the hare was nearly out of sight. The tortoise set off in his usual slow way.

When he reached the tree, the hare was so confident that he sat down to rest. But he soon fell fast asleep!

An hour later, he woke up and heard cheering in the distance. Leaping to his feet, he ran as fast as his legs would carry him, but the tortoise's head bobbed over the line a whisker before the hare's.

"Being quick on your feet is a fine thing, Mr. Hare, but slow and steady wins the race," said Mr. Tortoise.

The Fox and the Goat

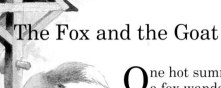

One hot summer, a fox wandered into an abandoned garden. Before he knew what was happening, he had tumbled into an old, deep well.

There was not very much water in the well, so the fox was quite safe at the bottom, but the sides were smooth and straight. The fox soon realized that he could not climb out.

The fox was beginning to think that he would never escape, when a foolish face looked over the top of the well.

"Hello down there!" boomed a voice. It was a goat.

The cunning fox at once saw his chance.

"My friend," he called, "come and share this lovely cool water with me!"

So the silly goat jumped into the well and drank the water. But before long, even the goat began to wonder how they could get out.

"Easy, my friend," said the fox. "Put your front feet as high up the wall as you can. I'll climb onto your back and jump to the top. Then I'll help you."

The goat did as the fox said. In seconds, the fox was out of the well and away. The poor goat was stuck.

Like the well, the moral of this story's deep: remember to look before you leap.

Puss in Boots

Once there was a miller with three sons. When he died, he left his mill to the eldest and his donkey to the middle son. To the youngest he left the cat that caught mice at the mill.

"How are we going to make a living?" sighed the youngest son.

"Don't worry," said the cat. "Give me a pair of your old boots and a bag." The miller's son did as Puss asked. The clever cat put some lettuce leaves in the bag and left it in a field. When a little rabbit came out and nibbled at the leaves, Puss ran out and caught it.

Then the cat set off to see the King.

"Your Majesty," said Puss, "Please accept this present of a fine rabbit."

The King was amused by the cat. "Who is your master, Puss?" he asked.

"My master is the Marquis of Carrabas," said the cat grandly.

One day the cat told his master to go for a swim in the river. "And you must pretend," he said, "that you are the Marquis of Carrabas."

When the King came past in his carriage, he saw Puss running around.

"Oh Your Majesty," cried Puss, "my master's clothes have been stolen!" (In fact, Puss had hidden them himself in some bushes nearby!)

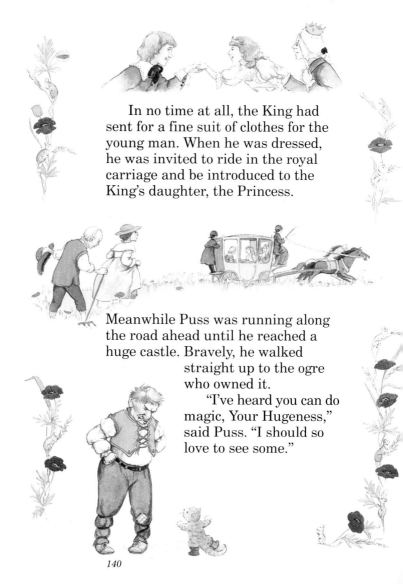

In no time at all, the King had sent for a fine suit of clothes for the young man. When he was dressed, he was invited to ride in the royal carriage and be introduced to the King's daughter, the Princess.

Meanwhile Puss was running along the road ahead until he reached a huge castle. Bravely, he walked straight up to the ogre who owned it.

"I've heard you can do magic, Your Hugeness," said Puss. "I should so love to see some."

The ogre laughed and turned himself into a lion!

"Hmm," said Puss, "but could you become something very small?"

In a second, the ogre turned himself into a mouse. At once, Puss pounced!

When the King arrived, Puss was ready. "Welcome to my master's home, Your Majesty."

The King was very impressed and so was the Princess. Before long she and the miller's son were married and they and the clever cat lived happily ever after.

Town Mouse and Country Mouse

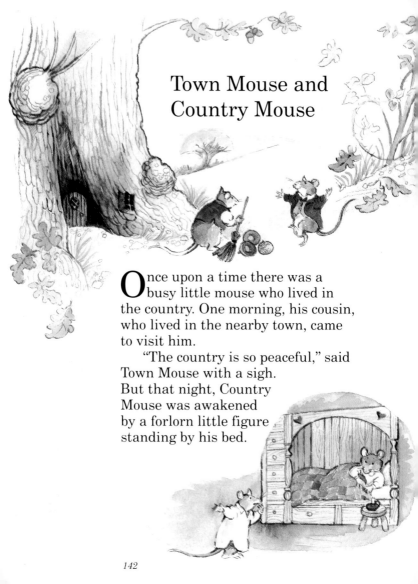

Once upon a time there was a busy little mouse who lived in the country. One morning, his cousin, who lived in the nearby town, came to visit him.

"The country is so peaceful," said Town Mouse with a sigh. But that night, Country Mouse was awakened by a forlorn little figure standing by his bed.

"Oh cousin," said Town Mouse. "I'm so frightened. There are horrible rustling and scurrying noises outside."

Country Mouse listened. "Those are just ordinary country sounds," he said. "You'll soon get used to them."

The next day, Country Mouse was busy as usual, picking berries and seeds to store for the winter. But Town Mouse did not want to work.

In the afternoon, Country Mouse made a picnic for his cousin. But Town Mouse was frightened of the big cows and horses in the field.

"Come back to town with me," he said to his cousin. "You'll love it there."

So Country Mouse set off with
Town Mouse. After a long day's
journey, they reached the big house
where Town Mouse lived.

"Isn't it splendid?" yelled Town
Mouse. But Country Mouse could not
hear him because of the traffic.

The mice had all the food they
could eat from the pantry. But
Country Mouse found it too rich.
"I think I'll go to bed now," he said.

But he didn't get a wink of sleep!
The streetlights kept him awake all
night. And next morning, Town
Mouse had to save his cousin from a
hungry cat! It was the last straw.

"Thank you for having me to
stay," said Country Mouse, "but I'm
going home to my old oak tree!"

Good Morning, Farmer!

One morning, a farmer set out from the farmhouse on his rumbling red tractor.

"Cluck, cluck!" said the hens. "Where are you going?"

"Oink, oink!" snuffled the pigs. "Are you going to market?"

"Baa, baa!" bleated the sheep. "Are you off to the hay field?"

"Honk, honk!" called the geese. "Are you going far?"

"Woof, woof!" barked the dog. "Aren't you taking me too?"

"And *where* are you going?" they snuffled and honked and barked.

But the farmer just smiled and chewed on a straw.

146

"Meow, meow!" cried the cat. "Are you going to collect something?"

"Quack, quack!" said the ducks. "Are you going to the river?"

"Moo, moo!" called the cows. "Are you going to the dairy?"

And all together they meowed and quacked and mooed. "Where *are* you going? Please tell us *now*!"

The farmer gave a smile as wide as the farm.

"With all this noise, I should think you could guess," he chuckled. "I'm off to town to buy some earplugs, of course!"

The Ant and the Grasshopper

Long ago on a sunny hillside, there lived an ant and a grasshopper. The grasshopper was a handsome insect with a glossy green coat. All day long he sat in the sun and made music, filling the hillside with his summery sounds.

"I don't believe that winter will ever come!" he chirruped.

The ant was small and dark. She bustled about every day, collecting grass seeds to store in her nest. "

"Oh yes, it will!" she said.

But soon the leaves began to fall from the trees. It grew colder and colder. At last one day, feathery flakes of snow began to fall across the hillside.

The ant was snug in her nest under a stone. She had enough food for the winter. Outside she heard a faint sound. It was the grasshopper.

"Dear Ant," he croaked. "Please give me some food."

But the Ant was firm. "I'm sorry," she said. "I need this food for my family."

A thick layer of snow settled over the hillside, and the grasshopper was heard no more.

The Little Red Hen

Once there was a little red hen who found some grains of wheat. She carried them off to the farmyard.

"Who will help me to plant this wheat?" she asked.

But the cat said, "Not I!"

And the rat said, "Not I!"

And the pig said, "Not I!"

"Then I shall plant it myself," said the little red hen. And so she did. By the end of the summer the wheat was high and golden.

"Who will help me harvest my wheat?" asked the little red hen.

"Not I!" said the cat.
"Not I!" said the rat.
"Not I!" said the pig.

"Then I shall harvest it myself," said the little red hen. And so she did.

When the little red hen asked for help to take her wheat to the miller and to the baker, it was the same story. She did it all by herself and baked the flour into beautiful brown loaves.

Then she said, "Who will help me to eat my bread?"

"I will!" said the cat.

And "I will!" said the rat.

And "I will!" said the pig.

"Oh no," said the little red hen. "I shall eat it all myself." And so she did.

The Elephant and the Mouse

Once there was a huge elephant who lived in the forest. He crashed along on his big, flat feet.

But one morning, as the elephant trampled across a clearing, he heard a tiny squeaking sound.

"Oh please," said a tiny voice, "please be careful! You're standing on my tail!"

Trapped by the elephant's foot was a very small mouse.

"I'm sorry," said the elephant. "I'll be more careful in the future."

From that day, the elephant always made sure that he was not stepping on a tiny creature. In fact, he was so busy being careful that he did not notice the hunters creeping up on him. Soon he was trapped in the hunters' net.

As he sat there sadly, the elephant was astonished to hear a tiny voice.

"One good turn deserves another," squeaked the little mouse. And she gnawed through the net. With a happy trumpeting sound, the elephant broke free!

The moral of this story is clear. If you help other people, they will help you!

The Wolf and the Seven Little Kids

Once upon a time there was a mother goat who had seven little kids. One day the mother goat had to go into the forest to find some food, but before she went, she spoke seriously to her seven children. "My dears," she said. "While I am gone you must not open the door to anyone, especially Mr. Wolf. You can always tell when he comes calling, because he has a gruff voice and rough, hairy paws."

The little kids promised that they would be very careful, and their mother set off for the forest. Before long there came a knock at the door.

"My dears," said a gruff voice, "it's your mother. Let me in!"

"You are not our mother," said the kids. They could see the wolf's paws on the window sill. "She doesn't have a gruff voice like you. Or rough, hairy paws! Go away!"

At this Mr. Wolf was very angry.

He hurried home and drank a honey drink to make his voice soft. Then he dipped his paws in white dough and ran back to the cottage.

The little kids heard his soft voice and saw his smooth white feet. "It *is* mother!" they cried and opened the door. In a flash, the wolf gobbled them all – except one.

When the mother goat came back, the little kid who had hidden told her everything.

"Right," she said, "I saw that old wolf asleep outside. Hurry!"

She crept up to the sleeping wolf and made a tiny hole in his fat tummy. Out jumped the six little kids! Then their mother filled the hole with stones and sewed it up.

When the wolf woke up, he staggered to the well for a drink, but his tummy was so full that he fell in and was never seen again.

The Ugly Duckling

There was once a mother duck who lived on a pond near a farm. All spring she kept her five big eggs warm under her feathers. One day, a faint tapping sound could be heard. One, two, three, four fluffy ducklings hatched from the eggs. Last of all, the largest egg hatched. The mother duck looked at her fifth duckling. He was a fine strong bird, to be sure, but he was *very* ugly.

With every day that went by, the strange duckling looked less and less like a neat little farm duck. The other ducks jeered at him and pecked him when his mother wasn't looking. The duckling was so unhappy that one day he ran away.

"I'll go and live with the wild ducks," he said to himself. But the wild ducks laughed. "Go away!" they quacked. "You'll frighten our ducklings."

So the ugly duckling ran away again. He walked wearily over fields and through woods. At last, as night was falling, he came to a cottage. He settled down on the doorstep out of the cold wind and went to sleep. In the morning, the old woman who lived in the cottage found the sleeping duckling. "You can stay," she said kindly, "with my hen and my cat."

But the hen and the cat had other ideas. They chased the duckling away. "You are no use at all," they said.

One afternoon in late autumn, the duckling saw some beautiful white birds flying overhead.

"If only I looked like that," he said.

Soon the duckling learned to fly. As he flew, he looked down and saw three of the beautiful white birds below on a lake. They were swans. As the duckling flew towards them, he caught sight of his own reflection and could hardly believe what he saw. He wasn't an ugly duckling at all! He was a swan! The other swans called to him kindly, "Welcome home!"

The Owl and the Pussy Cat

The Owl and the Pussy Cat went to sea
In a beautiful pea green boat:
They took some honey, and plenty of money
Wrapped up in a five pound note.
The Owl looked up to the stars above,
And sang to a small guitar,
"O lovely Pussy, O Pussy, my love,
What a beautiful Pussy you are,
You are, you are!
What a beautiful Pussy you are!"

Pussy said to the Owl, "You elegant fowl,
How charmingly sweet you sing!
Oh! Let us be married; too long we have tarried:
But what shall we do for a ring?"
They sailed away, for a year and a day,
To the land where the bong-tree grows;
And there in a wood a Piggy-wig stood,
With a ring at the end of his nose,
His nose, his nose,
With a ring at the end of his nose.

"Dear Pig, are you willing to sell for one shilling
Your ring?" Said the Piggy, "I will."
So they took it away, and were married next day
By the turkey who lives on the hill.
They dined on mince and slices of quince,
Which they ate with a runcible spoon;
And hand in hand, on the edge of the sand,
They danced by the light of the moon,
The moon, the moon,
They danced by the light of the moon.

Androcles and the Lion

Long ago there lived a young man called Androcles. He was owned as a slave by a rich Roman merchant, who treated him cruelly. One morning, Androcles ran away.

By midday, Androcles was too tired to run any further. He looked desperately for somewhere shady to hide and caught sight of the opening to a cave. Weak with hunger and exhaustion, he crawled inside.

Inside the cave, Androcles was terrified to see a fearsome lion. But the lion had a thorn in his paw and was suffering badly. Androcles could not bear to see such pain.

Bravely, he pulled out the thorn, and the lion padded softly away.

A few days later, Androcles was recaptured. He was dragged to the dungeons underneath the arena. This was a huge building where fights and shows were staged. Androcles knew what awaited him – to be torn apart by wild animals in front of thousands of people.

On the morning of the spectacle, two soldiers dragged Androcles from his cell and pushed him into the arena. The doors of the animals' cage opened and a fierce lion leaped out, roaring. Androcles fell to his knees, but the next moment he felt a rough tongue licking his face and looked up to see the lion that he had helped standing before him.

The crowd loved this amazing display and cheered until the Roman Governor announced that Androcles should be released.

The Nightingale

Long ago in China, there lived a great Emperor. His palace was as big as a city and around the palace there was a garden that stretched further than the eye could see. It was full of the loveliest plants and trees.

Among the trees of the Emperor's garden, there lived a little brown bird who was not very beautiful at all. It was a nightingale. When the nightingale opened her mouth and sang, the notes came trickling out like pearls from a silken purse.

One day the Emperor was told of the nightingale's song.

"Bring her to me at once!" he cried.

When she heard that the Emperor wished to hear her sing, the nightingale gladly went to the palace. Everyone who heard her wept at the lovely sound.

"Put the bird in a golden cage," said the Emperor. "I must hear this heavenly music every day."

But the poor nightingale hated to be imprisoned in a cage and sang no more.

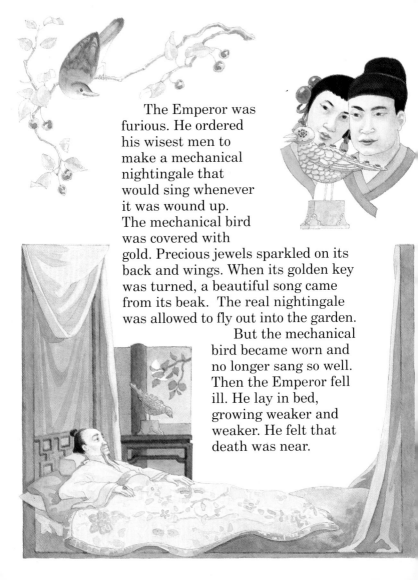

The Emperor was furious. He ordered his wisest men to make a mechanical nightingale that would sing whenever it was wound up. The mechanical bird was covered with gold. Precious jewels sparkled on its back and wings. When its golden key was turned, a beautiful song came from its beak. The real nightingale was allowed to fly out into the garden.

But the mechanical bird became worn and no longer sang so well. Then the Emperor fell ill. He lay in bed, growing weaker and weaker. He felt that death was near.

Alone in his room, the Emperor longed one last time to hear the nightingale. But he was too weak to turn the key. Then, from the window, the lovely song floated into the room. The real nightingale sat on a branch outside, singing her heart out.

In the morning, the Emperor was better than he had been for months. But he was a changed man. He ruled for many more years and the people, who had once feared him, now loved him for his kindness and wisdom.

Peter and the Wolf

Once there was a little boy who lived with his grandfather. His grandfather said, "Peter, you must never, ever go out of the garden and into the meadow. For the wolf may come out of the forest and eat you!"

Peter promised, but one sunny morning, he opened the garden gate and walked out. High in a tree was a little bird.

"Have you seen the wolf today?" asked Peter.

"No," sang the bird. "But you must warn that duck who has followed you."

The duck wanted to swim in the pond in the meadow. "Come and join me," she shouted to the bird.

"No," chirruped the bird. And she fluttered up and down on the bank. But she did not see a cat, creeping through the grass behind her.

"Look out!" called Peter, as the cat sprang, and the bird flew safely up into a tree.

"Thank you, Peter," she sang.

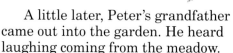

A little later, Peter's grandfather came out into the garden. He heard laughing coming from the meadow.

"Peter!" he shouted. "Come back into the garden at once!" Peter promised not to open the gate again.

Meanwhile, out in the meadow, a dark, shadowy shape crept out of the forest. It was the wolf!

The bird and the cat escaped into a tree. But the duck was too slow, and the wolf swallowed her whole!

Peter had seen everything from the garden. He thought of a clever plan to save the cat and the bird.

Peter found a piece of rope and climbed up onto the garden wall.

"Fly around the wolf's head and make him dizzy," he called to the bird. Distracted by the bird, the wolf did not see Peter dangle the rope down until he was firmly caught by the tail!

Just then some hunters came out of the forest. A grand procession took the wolf to the zoo.

"Quack! Quack!" Inside the wolf the duck stamped her feet with joy to think that she would soon be rescued.

No wonder the poor wolf wasn't feeling very well!

Noah's Ark

Long ago there was a very good man called Noah. He always tried to do what was right.

One day, God spoke to Noah. "I am going to wash away all the wickedness in the world, but you will be saved," He said. "I want you to build a huge boat, an ark, and put on it your wife and family and two of every kind of animal on earth."

Noah did as God had said, although passers-by jeered at him.

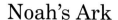

"You're welcome to join us if you like," Noah said, but the foolish people roared with laughter.

When the ark was finished, Noah called his sons and their wives and asked them to help him round up two of every kind of animal on earth.

"*Every* kind?" his youngest son asked.

"*Every* kind," said Noah firmly.

So two by two, the animals were led into the ark, and God shut its great doors.

Almost at once, black clouds
rolled across the sky and heavy rain
began to fall. Once it started, it just
didn't stop. Day after day it fell in a
steady stream. The ark
gave a lurch and a roll.

"We're floating!" cried
Noah.

For forty days and
nights the ark floated on
the floods. At last the
rain stopped.

"The floods will begin
to go down. We must find
land," said Noah.

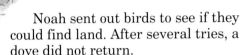

Noah sent out birds to see if they could find land. After several tries, a dove did not return.

"She has found a place to build a nest," said Noah. The next day, with a bump and a jolt, the ark settled on the top of a mountain.

Joyfully, Noah and his family and all the animals climbed out of the ark.

"Well done, Noah," said God. "I promise that I will never again destroy the world that I have made." And He made a rainbow, arching from the earth to the heavens, to remind us of His promise.

Chicken Licken

One day as Chicken Licken was walking along, an acorn fell on his head. "Oh my," said Chicken Licken. "The sky is falling in! I must go and tell the King."

So Chicken Licken set off. On the way he met Henny Penny and Cocky Locky.

"I am going to tell the King that the sky is falling in," said Chicken Licken.

"Then we shall come too," said Henny Penny and Cocky Locky.

So Chicken Licken and Henny Penny and Cocky Locky set off to find the King.

On the way they met Ducky Lucky and Drakey Lakey.

"Where are you off to?" they asked.

"The sky is falling in," cried Chicken Licken, "and we are going to tell the King."

"Then we shall come too," said Ducky Lucky and Drakey Lakey.

So Chicken Licken, Henny Penny, Cocky Locky, Ducky Lucky and Drakey Lakey set off to find the King.

On the way they met Goosey Loosey and Turkey Lurkey.

"Where are you off to?" they asked.

Chicken Licken told them.

"Then so shall we," said Goosey Loosey and Turkey Lurkey.

So Chicken Licken, Henny Penny, Cocky Locky, Ducky Lucky, Drakey Lakey and Goosey Loosey set off to find the King.

On the way they met a fox.

"Where are you going?" asked Foxy Loxy.

"The sky is falling in and we are going to tell the King!" they cried.

"Then follow me," said Foxy Loxy. "I know the way." So Chicken Licken, Henny Penny, Cocky Locky, Ducky Lucky, Drakey Lakey, Goosey Loosey and Turkey Lurkey followed Foxy Loxy. But he led them to his den, and his family ate them for dinner!

So all those foolish birds never did get to see the King. But then the sky didn't fall in either!

Among the Leaves

Who is that chirruping,
among the leaves?
"I am," said a sparrow.

Who is that
buzzing, among
the leaves?
"I am," said a fly.

Who is that shining,
in a pool among
the leaves?
"I am," said a fish.

Who is that scuttling,
among the leaves?
"I am," said a beetle.

Who is that hooting,
among the leaves?
"I am," said an owl.

Who is that croaking,
among the leaves?
"I am," said a raven.

Who is that singing,
among the leaves?
"I am," said a lark.

Oh, there is so much
to be heard and seen,
Among the leaves
so green, so green.

A Present for Percy

Sometimes it is difficult to find a present for a friend. Percy's friends had that problem every Christmas.

That pig did nothing all day but watch television! He didn't read books and he didn't play games. In fact, most days he didn't even get dressed! No, Percy just sat in his chair and watched and watched...

One year, Percy's friend Bella had an idea.

"Here's an exercise tape, Percy," she said.

And Percy did watch that tape, over and over again. But he never once stirred from his chair!

Perhaps this year, Percy will change his ways. For no one has bought him anything!

To Santa

The Three Billy Goats Gruff

Once there were three billy goats called Gruff. They lived in the mountains, searching for the fresh, green grass they loved to eat.

One day the three billy goats Gruff stood on a hillside and looked across a river. There was the freshest, greenest grass they'd ever seen. The goats trotted along the river until they came to a bridge.

"The bridge may not be very strong," said the smallest billy goat. "I will go first to make sure."

Now under the bridge lived a wicked old troll. When the smallest billy goat Gruff's hooves went *trip, trap* on the wooden planks, the troll peeped over the edge of the bridge.

"Who's that trip-trapping across *my* bridge? I'm a troll and I'm going to eat you for my dinner!" he roared.

But the goat replied, "I'm the smallest billy goat Gruff. My brother will be tastier than me."

So the troll let the
smallest billy goat Gruff go
trip-trapping on across the
bridge and onto the fresh, green
grass on the other side.

Next the middle-sized goat began
to cross the bridge. When he was in
the very middle, the ugly old troll
popped up again.

"Who's that trip-trapping across
my bridge?" he roared. "I'll eat you up!"

But the middle-sized billy goat
replied, "Wait for my brother.
He is much bigger!"

So the greedy troll let the middle-sized goat go.

Now the biggest billy goat Gruff had seen everything that had happened and he smiled to himself. His big hooves went *trip, trap* on the wooden planks. This time the troll jumped out and stood on the bridge.

"Who's that trip-trapping on *my* bridge?" he shouted. "Dinner at last!"

"I'm the biggest billy goat Gruff of all," came the reply. He lowered his horns and CHARGED!

With a great roar, the troll flew up into the air and down into the river below. The water carried him away, never to be seen again, and the billy goats Gruff lived happily ever after.

The Sly Fox and the Little Red Hen

Once there was a little red hen who had a neat little house in the woods. Her home kept her safe from the sly fox who lived nearby.

One morning the little red hen went into the woods to collect some sticks for her fire. She didn't know that as she worked, the sly young fox ran quickly into her house and hid behind the door.

When the little
red hen hurried
home with her
sticks, the sly young
fox jumped out!
Squawking with
terror, the little red
hen flew up to the
roof and perched on
a rafter.

The sly young
fox laughed. "You
can't escape from me
so easily, Little Red
Hen!" he said, and
he began to chase
his own tail around
and around the room. The little red
hen watched until she became so
dizzy that she dropped off her perch.

That was just what the sly young
fox had planned. He put the little red
hen into a sack and set off for home.

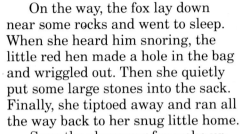

On the way, the fox lay down near some rocks and went to sleep. When she heard him snoring, the little red hen made a hole in the bag and wriggled out. Then she quietly put some large stones into the sack. Finally, she tiptoed away and ran all the way back to her snug little home.

Soon the sly young fox woke up and set off once more. The little red hen felt heavier than before!

When he reached his den, the fox's mother was delighted.

"The water is boiling, my clever boy," she said. "Throw her in at once."

With an enormous splash, the stones fell into the boiling water. The water splashed all over the two foxes and gave them such a fright that they ran away, leaving the little red hen to live happily ever after.

CHRISTMAS STORIES AND RHYMES

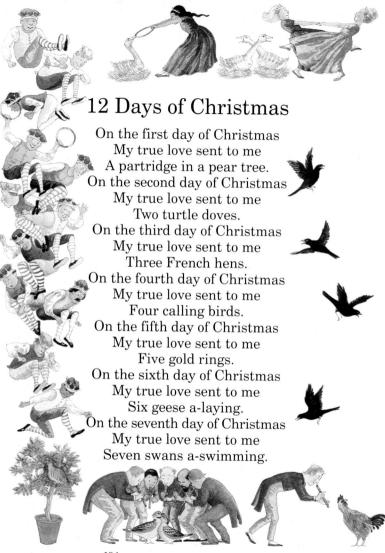

12 Days of Christmas

On the first day of Christmas
My true love sent to me
A partridge in a pear tree.
On the second day of Christmas
My true love sent to me
Two turtle doves.
On the third day of Christmas
My true love sent to me
Three French hens.
On the fourth day of Christmas
My true love sent to me
Four calling birds.
On the fifth day of Christmas
My true love sent to me
Five gold rings.
On the sixth day of Christmas
My true love sent to me
Six geese a-laying.
On the seventh day of Christmas
My true love sent to me
Seven swans a-swimming.

On the eighth day of Christmas
My true love sent to me
Eight maids a-milking.
On the ninth day of Christmas
My true love sent to me
Nine drummers drumming.
On the tenth day of Christmas
My true love sent to me
Ten pipers piping.
On the eleventh day of Christmas
My true love sent to me
Eleven ladies dancing.
On the twelfth day of Christmas
My true love sent to me
Twelve lords a-leaping, eleven
ladies dancing, ten pipers piping,
nine drummers drumming, eight
maids a-milking, seven swans
a-swimming, six geese a-laying,
five gold rings, four calling birds,
three French hens, two turtle doves
and a partridge in a pear tree.

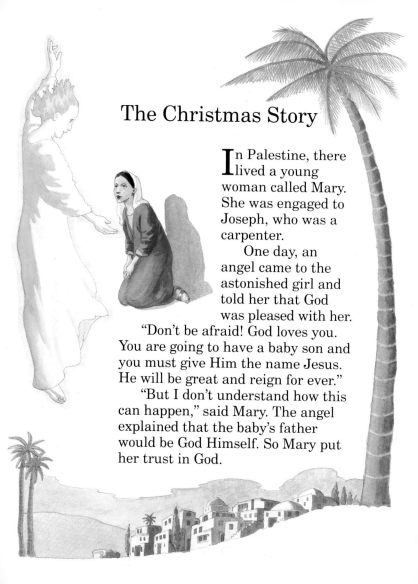

The Christmas Story

In Palestine, there lived a young woman called Mary. She was engaged to Joseph, who was a carpenter.

One day, an angel came to the astonished girl and told her that God was pleased with her.

"Don't be afraid! God loves you. You are going to have a baby son and you must give Him the name Jesus. He will be great and reign for ever."

"But I don't understand how this can happen," said Mary. The angel explained that the baby's father would be God Himself. So Mary put her trust in God.

When the baby was soon be born,
Mary had to travel with Joseph to
Bethlehem to take part in a census.
But none of the inns had any room.
At last a kind innkeeper let them
stay in his stable. That night, Mary's
baby, Jesus, was born. Mary laid
Him in a manger, on the hay left for
the animals to eat.

On the hills around Bethlehem, some shepherds were watching their sheep. Suddenly a bright light shone on them and a voice told them not to be afraid. The voice told the shepherds of the birth of Jesus. The trembling shepherds saw that the sky was filled with singing angels. At once, the shepherds hurried to Bethlehem to see the baby Jesus.

Far away, wise men also saw the bright star. They knew it was a sign that a great King had been born.

The wise men followed the star. They thought that the new King would be born in a palace, and they visited King Herod in Jerusalem. But Herod asked them to tell him when they found the King. He planned to kill the baby as soon as possible.

At last the star stopped above the stable where Jesus lay. The wise men gave Him gifts of gold, frankincense and myrrh. Then God sent dreams to the wise men and Joseph, warning them of Herod's plan. The holy family fled to Egypt and safety.

Silent Night

Silent night, holy night,
All is calm, all is bright
Around yon Virgin,
Mother and Child,
Holy infant,
So tender and mild.
Sleep in heavenly peace,
Sleep in heavenly peace.

Silent night, holy night,
Shepherds quake at the sight;
Glories stream from heaven afar,
Heavenly hosts sing hallelujah.
Christ, the Redeemer, is born,
Christ, the Redeemer, is born.

The Little Match Girl

One cold and bleak New Year's Eve, a poor little girl, trying to sell matches to buy herself a crust of bread to eat, shivered in a doorway. No one wanted to stop as they walked quickly by. Some did not even see her bare feet and ragged clothes.

When the streets began to empty and the lamplit windows called home the last passers by, the little match girl struck one of her precious matches to try to keep warm.

It seemed as though a glowing fireplace appeared before her. With a little cry, she stretched her frozen feet toward it, but the match went out and the fire disappeared.

With shaking fingers, the little girl struck another match. Now it seemed as though she could see through the wall of the house opposite. There was a table piled high with good things to eat, but as she stretched out her hands, the match went out and the vision vanished.

With tears in her eyes, the little girl struck a third match. Now she seemed to be inside the room, sitting under a candlelit tree.

As the tree's lights faded, the little girl lit her last match. She saw her beloved grandmother smiling at her.

"Please let me stay with you for ever!" cried the poor girl.

At that the old lady gathered her into her arms and carried her gently into the sky.

The next day, passers by found the little girl. She had gone to a better home than any on Earth for her New Year.

Good King Wenceslas

One snowy night, good King Wenceslas looked out of his castle and saw a poor man, carrying a bundle of sticks through the snow.

"Who is that man and where does he live?" the King asked his page. The boy replied that he was a peasant, whose home was at the foot of the mountain, on the edge of the forest.

"Bring me food and drink and some logs for his fire," said the King. "We will go visiting."

So the King and his page
went out into the blizzard.
Soon the page called out, "Sire,
I cannot go any further!"

"Walk in my footsteps,"
replied the King. "Look, we
have arrived!"

The poor man and his
family had a wonderful
Christmas. They were not
the last to bless the name
of that saintly King.

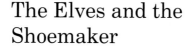

The Elves and the Shoemaker

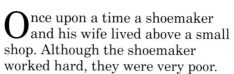

Once upon a time a shoemaker and his wife lived above a small shop. Although the shoemaker worked hard, they were very poor.

One day the shoemaker found that he had only enough money for leather to make one pair of shoes. He cut the leather out and left the pieces on his workbench before going to bed. The next morning, he was astonished to find that the leather had been made into a beautiful pair of shoes.

Still muttering in amazement, he put the shoes in his shop window. That morning, a very rich lady saw the shoes in the window and at once rushed inside.

"I simply *must* have those shoes!" she cried.

That afternoon, the shoemaker was able to buy leather for *two* pairs of shoes. As before, he cut out the leather and left it on his bench overnight. The next morning, two pretty pairs of shoes were waiting. So it went on, until the shoemaker and his wife were quite wealthy.

One night, just before Christmas, the shoemaker's wife said, "We still don't know who is helping us in this way. Why don't we stay up tonight and hide in your workroom? Then we will see what happens."

That night, the shoemaker and his wife saw two little elves run in and do all the work, then disappear.

The next morning, the shoemaker said to his wife, "Did you notice how ragged the elves' clothes were? Let's make them some little clothes and shoes to wear."

The shoemaker's wife thought this was an excellent idea. On Christmas Eve, the presents were finished. The shoemaker and his wife hid again to see what would happen.

At midnight the elves ran in as before. They were so overjoyed with their little suits and tiny shoes that they danced around and sang,

"We look so fine, as you can see,
We need no longer cobblers be!"

And with that they skipped out of the door. The elves never did return, but the shoemaker and his wife were happy for the rest of their lives.

Jingle Bells

Dashing through the snow
In a one-horse open sleigh,
O'er the fields we go,
Laughing all the way.
Bells on bobtail ring,
Making spirits bright.
What fun it is to laugh and sing
A sleighing song tonight!

Jingle, bells! Jingle, bells!
Jingle all the way!
Oh, what fun it is to ride
In a one-horse, open sleigh – hey!
Jingle, bells! Jingle, bells!
Jingle all the way!
Oh, what fun it is to ride
In a one-horse open sleigh!

The Best Present

"I want a *big* truck," said Charlotte,
"and I want some more carriages for
my train, and I want a box of
crayons, and I want…." The list
went on for some time, so that
Charlotte's mother, who was feeling
quite tired, stopped listening very
soon. Thank goodness Charlotte's
father was out in the town now,
picking up the present that they had
planned for their daughter.

"Now Charlie," said her mother, "sit down with me and listen. I really must tell you...." But just then Charlotte's dad arrived home with a huge package. "No looking, Charlie!" he cried, puffing upstairs.

"Can we play horses?" demanded Charlotte.

"Not now, Charlie. I don't really feel like it," said her mother, "and anyway, I still want to have a quiet talk with you."

But Charlotte didn't want to talk quietly. She wanted to run and jump and yell because that's how she felt with Christmas coming – *tomorrow*!

Much, much later, after quite a lot of running and jumping and yelling, Charlotte went to bed at last.

"Now if you hear any rustling and bustling in the night, you MUST NOT open your door," smiled her dad.

The next morning, Charlotte ran into her parents' room and suddenly stood quite still with her mouth open.

"Oh Charlie!" laughed her mother. "I don't think I've ever known you to stand so quiet and still for so long! Here's a present for all of us that came a bit earlier than I expected."

"This is the best present I've ever had!" said Charlotte. And, you know, she didn't even look at the big box waiting for her on the floor.

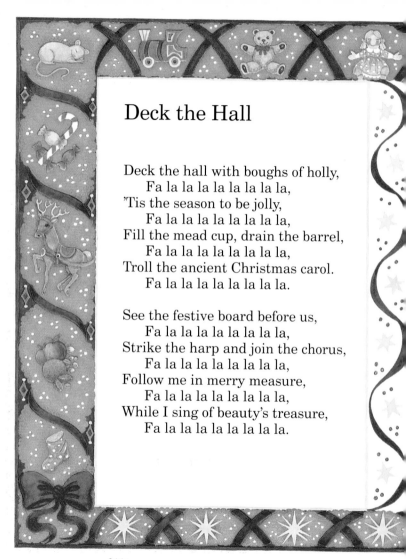

Deck the Hall

Deck the hall with boughs of holly,
　Fa la la la la la la la la,
'Tis the season to be jolly,
　Fa la la la la la la la la,
Fill the mead cup, drain the barrel,
　Fa la la la la la la la la,
Troll the ancient Christmas carol.
　Fa la la la la la la la la.

See the festive board before us,
　Fa la la la la la la la la,
Strike the harp and join the chorus,
　Fa la la la la la la la la,
Follow me in merry measure,
　Fa la la la la la la la la,
While I sing of beauty's treasure,
　Fa la la la la la la la la.

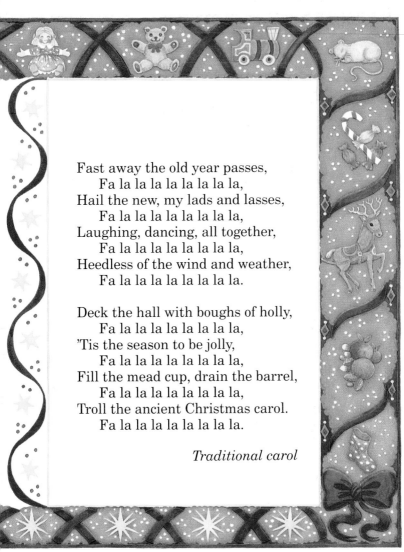

Fast away the old year passes,
    Fa la la la la la la la la,
Hail the new, my lads and lasses,
    Fa la la la la la la la la,
Laughing, dancing, all together,
    Fa la la la la la la la la,
Heedless of the wind and weather,
    Fa la la la la la la la la.

Deck the hall with boughs of holly,
    Fa la la la la la la la la,
'Tis the season to be jolly,
    Fa la la la la la la la la,
Fill the mead cup, drain the barrel,
    Fa la la la la la la la la,
Troll the ancient Christmas carol.
    Fa la la la la la la la la.

Traditional carol

Baboushka

Once there was an old woman called Baboushka who lived all by herself in a wooden hut in the forest. The nearest house was many miles away. Although Baboushka was very poor, she was happy.

One winter's night, as Baboushka sat sewing by her fire, she heard three knocks on her wooden door.

On the doorstep stood three very fine and important looking men.

"Come in, come in. You are very welcome on such a cold night," said Baboushka.

As she busied herself making the tea and finding some food, Baboushka asked the strangers where they were going.

"We are following a star that will lead us to the place where a new Prince has been born," said one man. "We do not know where it will stop."

"Who is this new Prince that you seek?" asked the old woman.

"He is a holy child," said the second man. "He is the Christ child, who will reign forever."

Baboushka's eyes widened as the third man showed her the precious gifts that had been brought for the new baby. "I wish I could see this holy child," she said.

"Then why not come with us?" the three men replied. "You are welcome."

"No, no," said Baboushka, sadly. "I am too old to go on a journey."

Soon the snow eased a little and the three men set off once more.

All night long, old Baboushka thought of the Christ child.

"I *will* go," she said. She packed a bag of toys for the new baby and set off across the snow. Poor Baboushka! She had waited too long. She could not find the three strangers. Some say that she is still searching, giving gifts to poor children on her way.

I Saw Three Ships

I saw three ships
Come sailing in,
On Christmas Day,
On Christmas Day,
I saw three ships
Come sailing in,
On Christmas Day
In the morning.

And they sailed into
Bethlehem,
On Christmas Day,
On Christmas Day,
And they sailed into
Bethlehem,
On Christmas Day
In the morning.

Traditional carol

The Real Reindeer

Across the ice of the Arctic Circle, a brown shape moved slowly. It was a real reindeer, separated from his herd in a snow storm.

One night, as he gazed into the sky, the reindeer saw something strange flying toward him. With a crash, it landed on the snow a few yards away, and a jolly man called out.

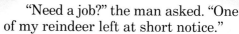

"Need a job?" the man asked. "One of my reindeer left at short notice."

The reindeer cleared his throat. "Er, well, the fact is ... I've never learned to, er, *fly.*"

The old man was doubled up with laughter. "Don't worry," he said. "I give on-the-job training. Come on!"

So the reindeer took his place with the others. "Hurry up!" cried the man in red, climbing into the sleigh. "This is a busy night for me! Three, two, one ... lift off!"

All that night, the sleigh flew over towns and villages, delivering presents. At last, the old man pulled off his cap. "Just one more present to deliver," he said.

Soon, the sleigh flew over a snowy landscape once more. "Will this be okay?" asked the old man. "There seems to be a few reindeer here already. Do you mind?"

"Mind? It's my *family*!" cried the reindeer joyfully. And he ran off to join them.

"Well, that's the last present delivered," chuckled Santa Claus. "See you next year!"

The Christmas Mouse

"Christmas is supposed to be fun,"
thought Jason gloomily. But there
was Great Aunt Gladys with her
mouth drawn in a thin line of
disapproval. Next to her were Aunt
Diana and Uncle Paul. They weren't
speaking to each other because their
car had broken down on the way over
and they couldn't decide whose fault
it was. Jason's sister Alison was
sulking because her boyfriend Mark
wasn't taking any notice of her. Mark
was silent. Jason's mother was tired
out and his dad was fast asleep.

Jason couldn't bear it any longer.

"Perhaps everyone would like to see my presents," he suggested.

"If there's something *quiet* you can bring, get that," said his mother.

So Jason went to his room and carefully lifted his new white mouse, Snowy, from her box.

Nothing had changed down in the dining room. Jason walked across to Great Aunt Gladys, his eyes on his cupped hands. That was why he didn't see the stool that she was resting her feet on.

In the confusion, everyone yelled together. But Jason was loudest, "Where's Snowy?"

There was a silence for a moment. "What?" asked everyone at once.

"Snowy, my mouse," explained Jason.

"Aagh," shrieked Jason's sister, throwing herself into Mark's arms.

"I *love* mice," cried Great Aunt Gladys, on her hands and knees.

"I'll catch it in my bag," yelled Aunt Diana.

"Stand clear, we need team-work," shouted Uncle Paul.

Five minutes later, the crisis and the gloomy silence were over. Mark and Jason's sister were giggling on the sofa. Uncle Paul beamed at his wife. "Using your bag was *brilliant*!"

"You organized everyone so well," she smiled back.

"I'm going to give that mouse the biggest hunk of cheese it's ever seen," said Jason's dad. "Merry Christ*mouse*, everyone!"

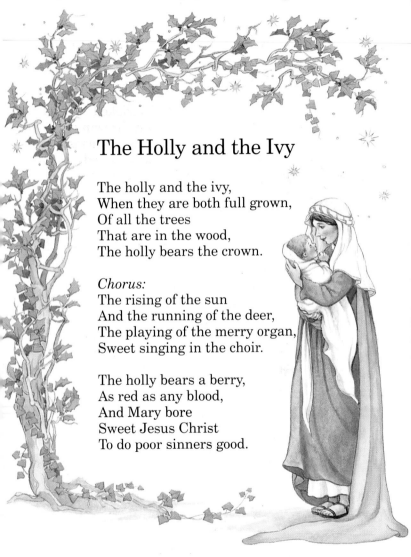

The Holly and the Ivy

The holly and the ivy,
When they are both full grown,
Of all the trees
That are in the wood,
The holly bears the crown.

Chorus:
The rising of the sun
And the running of the deer,
The playing of the merry organ,
Sweet singing in the choir.

The holly bears a berry,
As red as any blood,
And Mary bore
Sweet Jesus Christ
To do poor sinners good.

The Little Christmas Tree

Many years ago, deep in a forest, a little fir tree grew in a small clearing. All around it were huge trees, their tops reaching up toward the sky.

One day a truck with lots of men in it came along. It was time for the big trees to be felled and taken to the sawmill to be made into timber.

"All these are to go – except this little one, of course," said the foreman.

That night the little tree felt sad.

"I am sorry that you are going to be cut down," he said to the big trees.

The trees rustled their branches.

"Don't worry about us," they said. "Our tall, smooth trunks will be used to make all kinds of interesting things. But you will just be thrown away."

Then the little tree was even more sad. He gazed up at the night sky. "This is the last time that I shall see the stars," he thought.

The next morning, the big trees were felled. But the foreman did not pull the little fir tree up. He dug very carefully around him and lifted him, with a ball of earth around his roots.

229

Then he put the little tree in his truck and drove to his home. Three little children ran out and laughed.

"You've brought the Christmas tree!" they cried. "It's a lovely one!"

Today the little tree stands, tall and strong, near the house, and at night his branches almost seem to touch the stars.

We Three Kings

We three Kings of Orient are,
Bearing gifts we traverse afar,
Field and fountain,
Moor and mountain,
Following yonder star.

Born a King on Bethlehem plain,
Gold I bring, to crown Him again,
King for ever, ceasing never,
Over us all to reign.

Frankincense to offer have I;
Incense owns a Deity nigh:
Prayer and praising, all men raising,
Worship Him, God most high.

Myrrh is mine; its bitter perfume
Breathes a life of gathering gloom;
Sorrowing, sighing, bleeding, dying,
Sealed in a stone-cold tomb.

The Runaway Present

It was Christmas Eve, and all the Christmas presents were piled up under the tree. There were big ones and small ones, long, thin ones and round, fat ones.

The clock struck twelve in the quiet room. Suddenly, the pile of presents began to move slightly.

"Let me through! Excuse me! Please let me through!" said a voice.

At last a small present, wrapped in red and green, with a big bow on the top, struggled out of the pile.

It ran out of the door and off down the path, leaving tiny footprints in the snow.

All night long, the little present kept running. An owl sitting in an old oak tree looked down at the hurrying present below. Silently, he swooped down and picked up the present in his beak, carrying it back to his branch to examine it.

"Please don't eat me," cried the present. "I wouldn't taste good, honestly I wouldn't. And I'm in a hurry, you see."

"Too whoo!" hooted the owl. "Where to?"

233

"I got mixed up in the pile of presents under the Christmas tree. I should have been sent to the children's granny in the next town. She'll be so disappointed if I don't arrive. I really must try to get there by myself."

"Too whoo!" said the owl. "Well, flutter my feathers, that's the strangest story I've ever heard. If you give me directions, I'll carry you into town."

So the owl flew off through the trees, carrying the present in his beak.

Soon they arrived at the children's granny's house.

"Here I go!" said the present, jumping through the cat flap. "Bye!"

When you are unwrapping your presents next Christmas, look carefully to see if one of them is a little bit out of breath, for that will be a very special present indeed.

The Christmas Carol Mystery

"It's a mystery," said Vikky, "and someone must find out their secret." She was talking about Christmas carols. Every year two groups of singers went around the town, collecting money for charity. And every year the group from St. Mary's Church Choir, who sang like angels, collected less money than the group from the Youth Club, who made a really horrible noise, even when they sang easy carols.

"What we need," commented Janine, "is a spy! One of us should go around with the Youth Club."

"My cousin Jemima is coming to stay for Christmas," said Vikky. "They don't know her."

So that was what happened. Jemima went along to the Youth Club and volunteered.

Jemima reported back to St. Mary's.

"I think you should go out singing
on Wednesday night," she said.
"Before the Youth Club have a
chance to do it first."

The St. Mary's Choir spent all
Wednesday evening trudging the
streets, calling at every house. They
collected a lot of money.

On Thursday, Jemima set off to
join the Youth Club group.

"All right, team," said Gary, their leader, as they reached the first door. "One, two, three … Jingle bells…"

And there began the most awful noise that Jemima had ever heard. In seconds, a face appeared at the door and the noise stopped. "Another carol, sir?" asked Gary politely.

"No, no!" cried the man, throwing money at the choir.

And so it went on. Time and again, the Youth Club were paid handsomely to go *anywhere* else!

Jemima enjoyed herself so much that she never did tell her cousin how the Youth Club Choir succeeded. After all, there was room for both of them. You won't either, will you?

The Christmas Snowman

"It's the same every year," muttered the snowman. "Those children give me an old hat and a moth-eaten scarf and then forget about me. That man in the red coat and beard comes along and it's as if I don't exist. Ugh."

The next day the snowman wasn't any happier.

"I can feel a thaw in the air," he grumbled. "Drip, drip, my toes are melting already."

The snowman was still grumbling that night when there was a wooshing in the sky and a sleigh pulled by reindeer swooped down onto the snow.

"Oh no," said the snowman gloomily. "It's that man in red. What on earth does *he* want?"

The old man strolled up to the snowman.

"Could you look after this bag of presents for me?" he asked. "I'll leave the children a note to say that you've got it."

"It'll be safe with me, sir," said the snowman, proud to have a *real* job at last. He didn't close his eyes all night, as he guarded the bag.

In the morning, all the children from the house across the street came running over the snow to find their presents. Their dad came too with his video camera and filmed them opening their gifts.

"Fame at last!" thought the snowman. "That man in red never stays around long enough to become a star like me. Poor guy. I am lucky after all. The children would miss me as much as him if I were not here."

Well, almost!

In the Bleak Midwinter

In the bleak midwinter
Frosty wind made moan,
Earth stood hard as iron,
Water like a stone;
Snow had fallen, snow on snow,
Snow on snow,
In the bleak midwinter,
Long ago.

What can I give him?
Poor as I am?
If I were a shepherd,
I would bring a lamb;
If I were a wise man,
I would do my part;
Yet what I can I give him –
Give my heart.

Christina Rosetti

Mrs. Muddle's Present Puzzle

O ne morning, Mrs. Muddle said, "I will *not* get into the kind of muddle I did last Christmas. I will shop *early*."

All day she was busy shopping. Then she wrapped up *everything*. There was a train set for her nephew Jimmy, a scarf and hat for her brother Sam, a cookbook for stern Aunt Susan, sensible socks for Great Uncle Harry, roller skates for little Susie and a microscope for Susie's big brother, Tom.

Then Mrs. Muddle hid the presents under the bed.

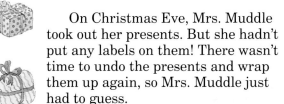

On Christmas Eve, Mrs. Muddle took out her presents. But she hadn't put any labels on them! There wasn't time to undo the presents and wrap them up again, so Mrs. Muddle just had to guess.

On Christmas day, Mrs. Muddle looked out and saw Great Uncle Harry roller-skating past.

"Best present I've had in years! Thanks!" he cried.

A second later, little Susie came past on *her* new roller skates.

"These socks are great! It doesn't hurt at all when I fall over! Thank you!"

The phone rang. It was her brother. "I've wanted a train set for years! And Jimmy loves his microscope," he said.

At the door, stern Aunt Susan beamed out from her hat and scarf.

"I was so fed up with *sensible* presents," she said. "These are such *fun!*"

"Well," said Mrs. Muddle, "what can Susie's brother Tom have got?"

Before she had time to work it out, Tom arrived.

"I've made you some cookies from my cookbook," he smiled. "It's a great present!"

Mrs. Muddle ate one of Tom's cookies. "I knew advance planning was the answer!" she laughed.

The First Noel

The first Noel the angels did say
Was to certain poor shepherds
In fields as they lay;
In fields where they lay,
Keeping their sheep,
On a cold winter's night
That was so deep.

Noel, Noel, Noel, Noel,
Born is the King of Israel!

They lookèd up and saw a star,
Shining in the East,
Beyond them far;
And to the earth it gave great light,
And so it continued both day and night.

And by the light of that same star,
Three wise men came
From country far;
To seek for a King was their intent,
And to follow the star
Wherever it went.

This star drew nigh
To the north-west;
O'er Bethlehem it took its rest,
And there it did both stop and stay
Right over the place where Jesus lay.

Noel, Noel, Noel, Noel,
Born is the King of Israel!